# Kubuki Love Palace

A
Novel by

# Rory Leon

RE-4
114 E. Indian River Road
Norfolk, VA 23523-1122

Cover design: Rory Leon Chatman Jr. (TJ); Anthony Lloyd (Nu-Nu); Rory Leon Chatman Sr.

Photography provided by Rod Cannon:
Hotrod@r2zphotos.com www.r2zphotos.com

Editing provided by Platinum Editorial Services

ISBN-13: 9780615382852

ISBN-10: 0615382851

First Printing: January 2012

10 9 8 7 6 5 4 3 2 1

This book in its entirety is a work of fiction. This is a product of the author's fictitious imagination; he has invented the characters, organizations, and events portrayed in this novel. Any resemblance to any actual events or person(s), living or dead, is purely coincidental.

Any and all of this books content are for entertainment only! Trying recipes or any other content of this book is at your own risk!

If you have purchased this book with a 'dull' or missing cover, you have possibly purchased an unauthorized or stolen book. If you got this from the flea market and it was one of the 5 for $25 deals, then someone is bootlegging my $#!+. Please immediately contact the publisher advising where, when, and how you purchased this book.

# Acknowledgments

First and foremost, I want to thank God! Although some of the contents may not be fitting for or in an agreement with the beliefs of those whom believe, talents are issued to each and every one of us. The Lord awards talents to us as He sees fit. I am thankful that the Lord has blessed me with many talents and I choose to do what he has for me to do with them. LORD, I thank you!

Second, to my wonderful family (Monique, TJ, Tré) who have been supportive and who are the inspiration for all that I do. Knowing that you are there when I need you keeps me focused to fulfill these dreams of mine. I owe it to God, and my parents that guided my way, which directed my future. Thank you for teaching me I can do anything that I put my mind to. My Brother(s) Doc, Skeets, Brian, Mike, "E", Octavious.

To my other family, and all of those that have their own place in my heart for each unique reason(s); Uncle William Johnson (Shooz) and Uncle Jerome Chatman (Beano) for giving me the hustle that is within in me! I truly appreciate all that you have done. Much love. Audrey Chatman (Mom), Sandra "R" Rawlins (Aunt), I appreciate the wonder-twin power that keeps me aligned; everyone should have the teaching of these twin angels. Uncle Rev. (Freddie Lee Chatman) for being honest with me while sharing the word of God (R.I.P.). I appreciate everyone; and there were too many Chatmans & Johnsons, along with extended family and friends to mention, but know that I thank you as well.

Special thanks to the persons involved with this project and those who gave input. "The keep it real authors" that shared their wisdom, experience, and didn't mind sharing the game.

Thanks Rod Cannon, for providing the lovely models for this book photography. "I appreciate your work!"

Thank you to the beautiful young lady on the cover—"What's your name?" I appreciate you volunteering yourself to make this happen. I wish you great success!

More importantly, to my readers, I hope you enjoy your ride to the Kubuki Love Palace; it was a true journey for me.

-Rory Leon

Models may submit photos to: kubukilovepalace@gmail.com

# Table of Contents

## Chocolate Crème

I was standing on the bus holding on to the safety bar, which kept me from falling over onto any of the many passengers. The bus was full and there were quite a few of us standing. I could feel something on my back, and had this I'm-being-watched feeling. I turned slightly, looking over my left shoulder, and there sat a pretty, young lady with a jacket sprawled across her lap, as if she were cold. I knew she wasn't cold because it was one of the hottest days in July. She just looked at me and blushed. Her blushing made me smile; I guess you could say that I blushed back. I turned my attention back toward the other passengers. I didn't want it to be obvious to her that I was very interested.

The bus was so crowded I could feel the hot breathe of the person standing behind me. My mind drifted into a state of lustful imagination. I began to add the body parts I wanted to see on her to make her the perfect woman for me. I began getting my game right in my mind; the game I was to spit at this sexual being. I wiggled, turned, and then stepped to one side to allow those people who were getting off the bus, by. Most of the people exited at the Janaf Mall stop. My stop was Military Circle Mall, which was up the road a bit. Janaf was more of a strip mall that was located across the street from Military Circle Mall.

I noticed she was still behind me, and if I was going to make my move, I had to do it quick. I was thinking I'm gonna sit next to her and introduce myself, then nervously go from there.

To my amazement, the woman I thought was there was gone! I mean she was there, but not what I'd envisioned. We neared our bus stop—I know it was our stop because she stood as we approached it. My mouth dropped open.

"Well, are you gonna say something or are you gonna allow your saliva to dribble on me?" she said.

"Excuse me. I am sorry. I didn't mean to . . ."

She stopped me in the middle of my begging for forgiveness.

"You don't have to apologize," she continued as we stepped off the bus. "It happens to me a lot."

Right then my heart softened on the spot. I felt like I didn't want to be like everyone else. I wasn't going to allow myself to judge a person before knowing the real them.

"Lemme start over. Hello. My name is Shooz. How are you?" I said.

She smiled at me, revealing a perfect smile.

"I'm fine, and my name is Rebecca."

"Rebecca, would you mind joining me for a bite to eat, somewhere inside the mall? Your choice. Maybe we can just sit and talk for a while."

"Sure," she said. Then she took my hand and we walked toward the mall. We talked over a meal at Piccadilly's, for what seemed like only half an hour, but ended up being two.

Man! Where did the time go?

She was pretty, bright, and sweet. Her personality made me forget my thoughts. I was totally engulfed in her after we talked. I never looked at her as being a midget again. She was a person—a beautiful person, who I wanted to grow with and love.

The phone rang disturbing my sleep. It was 12:36 AM. I knocked the phone to the floor reaching for it. "Shit!" I yelled as I clicked the lamp on to see where it had fallen.

"Hello?"

"Hi . . . Did I wake you?" Rebecca hesitantly replied.

"Yeah, but it's cool. What's up?"

"I just need to talk to someone. Are you alone?" she asked.

"Yeah."

"Do you mind if I come over?"

"No." Then I gave her the address.

It wasn't long before she knocked on my door. She was wearing a blue spandex dress that highlighted her curves. Her hair was in her usual ponytail. She wore blue shoes to match what she was wearing.

"Come in."

I had my PJs on. Just the bottoms, though, with a wifebeater that matched in color.

"Does my appearance offend you? If so, I'll change."

I didn't want to make her feel uncomfortable, but it didn't make sense to me to get dressed at 1:15 AM.

"No, I don't mind."

"I know you were asleep and I appreciate you getting up to talk with me. There is something bothering me, and I had nowhere else to turn. No one else I felt close enough to talk to, but you."

"It's okay," I comforted her.

She went on telling me about her day; and how her boss had called her an idiot, midget bitch and then yelled at her, "You're fired!" Tears began to flow down her cheeks. Her little hands covered her eyes. I pulled her close to me, hugging her and running my fingers through her hair. I gently kissed her forehead.

"Baby, don't worry. You'll find another job."

She raised her head up from my chest and we kissed for the very first time. I ain't gonna lie neither, with my eyes closed, it felt like kissing a woman my height. One thing leads to another and we began caressing each other's body. She was well-proportioned—fine as hell. I began to rise as my hands voyaged across her hardened nipples. I removed her straps with some assistance from her. I undid her bra, revealing breasts that made my mouth water. I took in the right one, with gentle caressing of the left. My hand left the mountain of passion and journeyed to the valley of pleasure. Keep in mind that it didn't take long considering her size.

At first she flinched; then she began to gyrate slowly. I could feel her through her clothes, but that wasn't good enough, I had to go under her 4T spandex dress. Her pussy was wet. With one hand, I removed her soaked panties. She lifted her leg so her panties would ease off, then I could feel her wiggling them off and flinging them with her foot toward the air.

With two fingers, I circled the sugar walls of her pussy, slightly dabbing the middle, wetting my fingertips and moistening the pussy's lips. She moaned, but could only lie there, because her arms were too short to reach my dick from the position I was in.

I took her dress off. Her body was smooth; her skin was the color of a Bit-O-Honey. Her clit looked like an entrance to a teepee or a hut. I started at her calf because I don't suck toes! With gentle kisses, I found my face in a pool of pleasure. My tongue traced the same pattern my finger did. I sucked her pussy while she rubbed my head with her stubby fingers. I stopped the motion of her hand 'cause that shit felt funny.

"Damn, you're sweet," I softly spoke, sucking her clit like I was sucking the meat out of a neck bone.

She gyrated gently. Her moan got stronger, her breathing heavier. I put my chin in it and moved it about smartly. She came on my chin like it was a stubby dick. I stood to my feet with my face feeling like a glazed donut. She stood also. She began removing my PJs; loosening the drawstring, then letting them fall like timber in the woods. She was patiently savoring the moment.

Slowly, she caressed my ass cheeks; then grabbed the brim of my MJ drawers. I stood and watched with anticipation. I could see my pre-cum shining on the tip of my shaft once she pulled them from around it. I stepped out of my drawers into a warm sensation.

"Ooh shit," I moaned.

She stood eye to eye with this Virginia black snake. I couldn't really see what was going on. All I know is the shit felt good. It was ten minutes before I saw my dick again. Her tongue ventured the shaft toward my ball sack. Her tongue slapped them around like a school bully. My dick looked bigger than usual. I guess it was because her hand was so small and her fingers couldn't reach all the way around it. This excited me more . . . I felt dominant.

"Lie on the bed," she said.

"Okay."

"You taste so good to me."

I relaxed on the bed. She mounted me in the 69 position and took me in her mouth again, licking and sucking the whole thing. I tried to return the favor, but her sweetness only came to my chest, so I played in it instead. My thumb circled her around or about her sphincter. Her wet pussy released juice, which ran down my chest.

I began to break the matrix, fingering her ass. She took my dick out of her mouth and laid her head in my lap. I have to admit I have fat fingers! She took my dick in her mouth again, this time moaning as she attempted to deep-throat it. Faster, her pace began jacking my dick like pumping water from a well. My finger went in and out of her ass slowly, but conquering the domain.

"Oh! I wanna taste you!"

"Oh, shit, that feels good!" she spat. "I think I am cumin', Shooz."

I could feel the commotion inside my nuts; the rambling feeling, escaping the foundation of my love.

"Oh, shit." That was me this time. I moaned like a bitch, "Ummm . . ."

The warmth of her mouth took me there. She drank from my spigot of love; she squeezed and pulled every drop of me into her mouth. She whimpered like a puppy being whooped! She wanted more. I took my finger out of her ass. It popped like I uncorked a bottle of champagne. She sucked the strength back into my weakened dick. She must have had something against my dick the way she handled it. She rubbed my nipples.

"Damn, you got a strong grip, girl," I said unbelievingly.

She just held on as tight as her little hands could as she climbed on top of me. Her pace was slow at first, but later quickened. She rose up, taking all of me out of her except the tip; then she ease down again. She was beautiful. Her eyes were closed and she wore a silly grin, with her bottom lip tucked neatly away.

Small beads of sweat escaped on to the tip of her nose and above her top lip. I was turned on! It was exciting to watch her enjoy our sex. She quickened her pace. "I'm about to cum," slipped out my mouth like a little bitch!

She screamed passionately, letting me know she was there, too. Rebecca dismounted before I could cum. She took me in her mouth once more.

"Oh, God!" I yelled out.

I grabbed a handful of sheets, trying to pull the springs out of the mattress. The muscles in my ass tightened. I could feel myself nearing climax; I gritted my teeth.

"It's coming!"

Before I knew it, my juices filled the wells of her mouth, some oozing out the sides.

"Umm," she said. "Sweet chocolate crème."

Then she licked her lips, ridding herself of her milk mustache. I was paralyzed briefly. I fell asleep and then two hours later, we went at it again. . . .

"DAMN, THAT CHOCOLATE CRÈME!"

## HAPPY BIRTHDAY, BABY

The limo driver waited outside my townhouse while I locked the door. He stood there in his white tuxedo, with a charcoal gray cummerbund and matching bow tie. He opened the door and greeted me, "Hi, my name is Derek James, and I am your driver for the evening."

"Hi, I am Kris," I replied to his greeting as he grabbed my hand and led me to my seat inside the limo. He then revealed a velvet covered box with a blindfold and instructions inside.

The instructions read: HEY, GIRL, THIS IS YOUR BIRTH-DAY PRESENT. SO, DO AS YOU'RE INSTRUCTED AND I PROMISE YOU A GREAT EVENING. LOVE, FRENCHY.

He placed the blindfold over my eyes, closed my door, and took his place behind the wheel. The ride began and I could only think of what I had just seen: a five-feet-eleven-inch black man with king features. His skin was brown like a penny! His lips were thin, his nose was slim, and he had a pair of walnut eyes that said things to me that words could not.

I liked the way his tux matched the Lincoln Navigator limo, and the scent of his cologne. Which I later found out was Casran. He said his brother sent it to him from overseas. His voice melted my heart and soul. I wanted him deeply. My thoughts began to make my nipples harden, my clit get moist. I touched my breasts gently and I licked my lips softly, with hopes that he was watching.

The limo began to slow to a stop, the door opened, and then I heard Frenchy. "Girl, how you doin'? Are you a'ight?"

The car began to move again. I said, "Girl, what the hell are you doing? Where we going?"

"Just chill. We gonna celebrate your birthday the right way!" she replied.

I whispered to her, "Do you know the driver?"

"He *is* cute!" Frenchy stated without answering.

In the back of my mind I was hoping that he was my birthday present. I visualized him undressing in front of me, very slowly, so my eyes could grace his body like lustful people do. His penis would harden from my gaze and he would approach me slowly, and I would take his hardened dick into my mouth. I would begin sucking him off like a porn star: licking and sucking, even taking his ball sack into my mouth, then vibrating my throat. He caressed the back of my head while I preformed this lovemaking art on him. I looked into his eyes to see the pleasure look upon his face that I'd put there.

"Hey! Dammit! What the hell you thinking about? You got all quiet and shit on me. And what's with all the grinning and shit?"

"Nothing, girl." I tried to play it off.

"Naw, you were thinking something." She laughed. "His name is Derek; I know him from work. Derek drives limousines part-time, so he agreed to do me a favor. So, I owe him one."

Frenchy made me a drink she called "Phuck It." She said after I had a few, I would say fuck it to anything! Carefully, I brought it toward my lips for a taste. It tasted like cherry-pineapple with a hint of coconut. I drank it like Kool-Aid. Dayuuum!

"Girl, that's the bomb! Fix a homegirl another one."

Moments later we stopped again, and Frenchy led me out of the limo. I went through a spinning door like those used at banks. "Watch your step!" she said, helping me up about three steps. I heard people in the background, but I couldn't place what type of environment I was in. Frenchy opened another door and we walked in. "Girl, take off your clothes," she said, as she began to unbutton my blouse.

I was nervous as I held her hand, keeping her from opening my blouse. "Is anyone here with us?" I asked. I wanted to assure myself that no one was in the place with us, and that this wasn't some sick joke she was playing.

"Naw! Girl, just take this shit off," she laughed, then continued, "You know I wouldn't do any silly shit like that!"

She reached at my blouse and undid each button slowly. With both hands she placed them on my breast and eased my top open and over my shoulders until it fell to the floor.

## Frenchy

*Dayuuum!* I thought to myself. *Her breasts are soft as hell.* I tucked my bottom lip underneath my teeth and enjoyed the moment. I unbuttoned her pants and put my hands inside her waistline and eased her pants off—softly. I rubbed my hands across her ass, removing her pants. Her panties slid down a little and I began to get excited with the whole thing. Her ass was round without blemishes, smooth vanilla-pudding skin tone, and her sweet scent smelled of Versace perfume.

I wanted to lick her navel up to her breasts; then circle each nipple gently, taking one in at a time, into my hot mouth. My breathing became shallow. I could feel the quivering of her body. I could tell she was getting cold. I wanted to blow some cool air across her clit.

## Kubuki Love

"What are you doing?" she asked.

I sensed that she knew my intentions, but I just played it off. "Relax, girl. It is a surprise."

With one hand placed behind her calf, I helped her step out of her pants. She stood there, unknowing of my next move. I disappeared into the closet section of the room; then returned with a box. I took the top off of the box and revealed a red dress that I had her step into. I eased her into the dress the same seductive way I eased her out of her clothes. She looked good, and that red dress embraced her vanilla skin sweetly. It was something else seeing the way the color red high-lighted Kris's complexion.

I was so wet my juices began to soak my panties. I put a pair of matching shoes on her to go with the out-fit. There was a knock at the door that threw me out of my thoughts of fucking Kris's sexy ass! I'm not sure she knows that I want to fuck her. Even though she is my friend, she'll get done!

I've had female friends—some say partners, I say associates. I also like my men. There is nothing like a dick. And ain't no pussy licking can beat a good stiff one! I wish men could make me feel the way a woman makes me feel with her touch, and how gentle she is with it. Women know how to touch other women and where to touch us to get the maximum pleasure out of orgasms. I've never cum multiple times with a dick, but I have with my associate. She spent quality time with the "little man in the boat," sucking, licking, stroking him—making him her personal task.

Then she gave me the "bowling ball." Oh, my God! The bowling ball was the shit! She stuck one finger in my ass and her thumb rubbed the outer walls of my vagina. Then she inserted her thumb and began to massage the little man with her tongue. She worked that bowling ball shit until I needed an orthopedic doctor to unlock my curled toes! I began to cum repeatedly. I mean, she wouldn't stop licking and probing my erotic zone. She raised her head above my surface and said, "Your cum tastes sweet, baby." And my mind had a reaction all its own. There was something about words spat during sex that sent me into another world. My whole body quivered, my sugar walls vibrated with emotion, my juices trickled down my inner thighs.

I felt so relaxed it took me a few seconds to regain my composure. I have never felt such magic. We had toys we used but nothing—and I mean nothin'—could replace the way she touched me. But every once in a while I need a dick. A real DICK!

## Kris

There was a knock at the door. "Hold on, girl. I have to answer the door," Frenchy said. Footsteps were all I heard, then some rumbling of plates, dishes, and silverware. I was waiting for them to yank the blindfold off and yell "happy birthday!" at any second, but that never happened. "Come on, let's go," Frenchy said.

She grabbed my hand and led me into the hall, then back out to the limo. Again, his cologne sexed my mental, his voice seduced my body, and his touch sent chills across my arms. "Thanks," I said, as he helped me into the limo

"Sure. And please, love, watch your step," he replied. His hands were soft, Not like those of a labor working man, but of a man that had a cushioned job. I tried to feel for a ring on his hand, because with the blindfold I couldn't see if he was wearing one or not.

"Fix me one of those Phuck It's!"

Frenchy laughed. "Girl, you gonna be fucked up."

It was my birthday and it didn't matter to me because I didn't have to work the next day, anyway. This Phuck It was colder than the first one. I suppose she had left it in the refrigerator.

"Where did you get this? Did you make it?"

"Derek made it. He used to bartend a couple of years back." I was liking him, and I didn't even know him. But I wanted him all the same. I was feeling like, fuck it, I ought to go for it! I wanted to taste him.

All of a sudden, the limo stopped and Frenchy eased the blindfold off of my head. The light was blinding and it took a second for my eyes to readjust. There were flowers and a card on the seat in front of me, with a box of chocolates. I saw a pitcher of the Phuck It being chilled on ice. The stereo was playing Frankie's CD. The song playing was "If I Had You." That is just what I was thinking! Derek opened the door and rolled out the red carpet. We were at Freemason Abbey Restaurant, located in the downtown Norfolk area.

The dress I was wearing was nothing short of being the bomb diggy! I mean it was slammin'! The way it fit around my curves—umph! It was something that I would have never bought for myself. People were walking by looking at us as we stepped out of the limo, but I was only concerned about Derek noticing how I looked.

"Girl, I like this dress!" Frenchy admired.

"Thank you! You know that I would have never bought this for myself."

"You're welcome, girlfriend!" Frenchy said with a smile. Frenchy was wearing a nice beige dress with a brown belt that made her dress look like it was two pieces instead of one. She was looking pretty good with her little five-foot-five-inch self. Frenchy's hair was in a ponytail and she had the diva look with a pair of sun-glasses on. Her lips were nicely moistened with lip-gloss. She never wore lipstick! I was always envious of her because guys would go crazy over her lips and say she had a nice pair of DSLs. That meant Dick Sucker's Lips! I have to agree with them, she had a set of soup coolers and she kept them wet. Looking like Dunlop's with Tire Wet on them.

That thought made me laugh to myself.

We walked in the Freemason restaurant and were seated by the hostess. "Hello. How many in the party? Do you have a reservation?"

Frenchy said yes to her; then gave her the regis-tered name. My eyes perused our surroundings as we walked to the table where we were seated.

"This is nice! Frenchy, you didn't have to do this, girl. However, your birthday is next, maybe you're send-ing hints?"

"Are you ladies ready to order?" the tall, skinny, Kobe Bryant-looking gentleman with a fro and cocoa brown skin, asked.

Before I could speak, Frenchy said, "Dante, hook us up with the Dante's Special." Then she winked at him. He returned moments later with a bottle of the finest wine in the place.

"I will bring your food momentarily."

He meant just that! He returned with a feast! We had steak with potatoes and sour cream. There was salad, bread, and vegetables.

I was like, "Dayuuum, that was quick!"

Frenchy just laughed and said, "Enjoy."

We ate like stowaways for the next thirty minutes. Frenchy pulled out her cell phone to make a call. "Va-moose, mi Negro!"

"A'ight, girl, you ready to go?" she then asked me.

"Yeah," I said.

Dante brought the fake check. They kissed each other's cheek like French people do. "Bye, love," he said sensually in her ear.

"You know Kobe, too?" I asked when we got back to the limo. "And we didn't even pay for that meal." No words were said by her, she just smiled at me with those shiny-ass lips. She didn't answer any of my questions until later that evening.

The glass of Phuck It was calling me. We cruised by the beachfront of Virginia Beach before heading back the other direction to watch Nickel and Dime at the Willet's Hall in Portsmouth.

The play was funny as hell; Especially after the Phuck It kicked in. "Ha, ha, ha, ha," I laughed hysterically, almost slobbering when the one guy recited to his woman a *Bitch,-You-Ain't-Shit!* poem.

Bitch, you ain't shit!

Gon' leave a nugka to sample dick!

Come telling me some stupid shit like,

If you let something go

And it returns to you, then it yours.

No, bitch, yooooz stillza, ho!

Nah, gets your bags and pack your shit

Gon' stank ho and sample dick!

I mocked him mocking his girlfriend.

"Ha, ha, ha, ha, ha. Let's go clubin'," I told Frenchy.

By the time we made it in the club, the Phuck It had kicked in good. We were only there for a quick minute. I walked in and straight over to a fine-ass broth-

15

er and started dancing with him on the dance floor. He was dancing with himself at first, for what reason I don't know. My body felt loose and limber. I began to grind on him; then I turned and dropped it like it was hot! I brought it back up like a stripper and teased his hardened penis with a few ass bounces.

Frenchy couldn't believe my forwardness, but she came right over and joined in—we sandwiched that brother! I know he felt he was the shit, to have us all over him like that. Frenchy was like that. What I mean is she danced with both of us. Her hands invaded our privacy; her ass cheeks gyrated the middle of our well-being! She sexed our mental with seductive stares. She was mind fucking us! I felt like she was the requested partner in a threesome. Dayuuum, that Phuck It had me going. I know someone was rubbing my body. I don't know if it was him or her, but that shit felt good as hell!!!

"Girl, I gotta sit down!"

"Naw, let's go!" she said. Frenchy took my hand and led me to the door of the club. The guy was left standing there like, *what just happened?*

My legs weren't under me too well, so I had to tell Frenchy to slow down her stride, before I embarrassed myself by falling. I wanted some sex now; I didn't care where it came from. I had in my mind that I was going to proposition Derek when we got back to the limo. I wanted his fine ass in more way than one.

The limo was waiting for us outside. Derek had the red carpet rolled out. "Final destination," Frenchy said to him as we began to climb in.

I reached out and grabbed his ass. *Fuck it*, I was feeling bold. "I want you," I told him. He just smiled at me with those little lips.

"I want you, too, but I am married, love."

Dayuuum! Why are all the fine ones taken, and the ones that are not are gay or in jail? I climbed my drunk ass in and accepted my losses. Frenchy buzzed Derek once he climbed into the driver's seat. He rolled the privacy window down.

"Put that "Oooh Boy!!" mix CD in that you made."

He nodded then complied. The first song was Usher's. I closed my eyes and leaned back into the plush leather interior that surrounded my delicate frame. I felt a sensation come over me. I felt passion. I felt moist. I—I—I felt Frenchy kissing me!

My mind was yelling no, but my body was saying yeah. She explored my full 36Ds with her fingertips; she stroked my kitten shortly after. I rose back in the seat and said, "Wait a minute, hold up a second." My words were said out of satisfaction. My words had little to no effect because they were spoken softly. She kept kissing and rubbing my breasts, and she eased them from my dress and began to use her DSLs like a champ.

"Wait—wait!" I said in a sexual tone. "What are we doing? We are best friends?" I had only been with another woman once before.

She said to me, "I feel as if it was meant to be. It feels right! It feels good. Sometimes you have to do what you feel."

We drove up to the front door of the Norfolk Marriott in downtown Norfolk. The door opened. "Come on," she said.

"Thank you, love," she said to Derek.

"You ladies have a good evening, and happy birthday, Kris."

"Thank you, Derek," I replied.

She had a room on the 23rd floor overlooking the waterside. The view was beautiful at night and you could still see people walking around, enjoying one another's company.

I noticed the clothes that I wore earlier were hanging up in the closet. The room was beige and rose with cherry wood furniture: two beds, a refrigerator, and a wet bar. She had more Phuck It up in the refrigerator. She said it was for her for later. She poured some in a little glass for the both of us. She kissed my lips softly. I understood the whole DSL thing now! I know now why guys like big-lip women, because her lips were cushions—dick pillows!

She undressed me the same way as she did earlier. I understood the passion in her fingers when she ran them across my body again, for the second time. She squeezed my breasts, then suckled the both of them. She eased my panties off and laid me down across one of the beds in the room, and began to gently kiss my body.

The whole thing was too much for me at first, but I was like fuck it! She rubbed my entire body with a peaches and crème edible lotion. She started eating the lotion from my peach! I caressed my breasts as her lips danced forbiddingly across my sugar walls. I quivered softly as she lapped up my juices.

Frenchy worked the middle for quite some time. I climaxed three times before I pulled her off to return the favor. Her brown skin was soft, her breasts just the right size. I tried some of that lotion. It was pretty-tasty. I traveled down to her shaved delight. I tickled the man in the boat, while I circled her clit with my fingers. I stroked her pussy with my tongue and fingers until her body shook like she had been hit with a Taser gun.

After we lived as lovers, she washed my body. I felt like a queen on Fantasy Island. I know it was my birthday; nonetheless, she was my present that night.

I truly had a happy birthday that night. Thank you, Frenchy!!!

## Hot Tub

Midnight . . .

The music was loud as a motherfucker! The receptionist from the hotel's lobby had called, asking politely for us to turn the music down to a more friendly level. A few of the other guests had called them, complaining about the level of noise we were carrying. As much fun as we were having, I didn't feel that I had to comply, but I did anyways. You know how black folks do when we party hard. There was about fifteen of us talking, consuming alcohol, and waiting on the man of the hour. He was late as hell.

The entertainment showed and retired to the bathroom to put on outfits for the night's event. There were three lovely ladies: Crème, Diamond, and Karmel. Of coursethese were their stage or dancing names. Like I really gave a fuck what their real names were. We didn't need a name to go by because we recognized these ladies by their beauty!

I will say that their names fit them to a tee. Crème was light in complexion with green colored contact lens, and a seductive stare. Diamond was chocolate, sexy as a muthafucka, with a body like Sugar-Foot. She had outdone Crème in all aspects, and right then was number one in my eyes, but that remains to be seen.

Now, let us talk about the lady of the night—the treat for the man of the hour—Karmel. Tall, sweet and sensuous! She was the one who got along with all; her personality is flawless. Karmel is a relationship builder! She had all of the right words to say. When she entered the room, she grabbed my cheeks softly and said, "Hey, baby." It liquefied my heart. I longed till this day to hear her say those words to me again. She stood nearly six feet tall, had soft caramel skin, and that ass looked like two caramel apples.

Diamond was the first out to work the crowd. She danced for us as we caressed her with one-dollar bills. She saved everything for the man of the hour. That means she took off no clothes until he arrived. By the way, where the fuck is he?

Just then, Midnight's phone rang. "Hello. Yeah, a'ight! Hey, fellas, they are coming out the elevator now. They will be here in five-four-three . . ." he counted as he looked through the peephole in the door.

"Without further ado, I present to you the man of the hour: SUGA!!!!"

The girls rushed him as he entered the room like he was the pimp of the year, royalty or something. Suga smiled a wide smile as he perused the treats before him. "Hey, what's the occasion?" he asked.

Midnight spoke first, "Tonight we are celebrating Suga! And the next party will be for me, for being the blackest nugka in the room!"

Everyone laughed as Midnight sipped his cup of Hypnotic. Midnight was the loudest at all the parties; the center of attention with his fancy clothes, monies, and loud talking. The ladies always flocked toward him. He got his name because he was the blackest in the whole room, and he generally didn't come out until the midnight hour. He was Suga's right-hand man in Tampa. He had Suga's back, regardless. Midnight always provided the entertainment for gatherings of all sorts . . . this was his way of making his ends meet.

"Brother, tonight is your night!" Midnight said with a look of sincerity as he embraced Suga in a brotherly hug. All the others cheered in agreement.

"Thanks, bro," Suga smiled.

"Enjoy," Midnight whispered in his ear, as he released his hold.

"Now, pour that man a glass of Hennessy with a splash of his favorite!" Midnight yelled.

Diamond was the first to rub her very nicely shaped ass on Suga. She grinded her rear slowly, ensuring his attention was directed toward her. With one hand on his glass and his other on her ass, he wound his waist, then took a taste, stroking gently as his penis stiffened! Diamond reached back and squeezed his ass pulling it closer, intensifying their gyration.

Soft moans grew stronger as she simulated a climax. "Fuck me, Suga! Fuck me! Oh yeah, daddy! I like that. Do that shit! Fuck that ass!"

Suga's gyration turned into a pumping motion, his lips disappeared with concentration. Suga's face was filled with determination. Even the presence of Crème couldn't distract what he had already set his mind to.

Crème approached Suga from the rear, where she sandwiched him between herself and Diamond. She reached her hand around and grabbed Suga's stiffened penis. She rubbed it and stroked it through his sweat pants. Crème tucked her bottom lip in, and by the look on her face, she was pleased with what she held in her hand.

Midnight grabbed a handful of Crème's ass. She turned around and he put her breast between his big, moistened lips. She screamed in ecstasy, with one hand cupping the back of his head, bringing him forth to enjoy a mouth full of her beauty.

"It's a party!" Midnight yelled.

The ladies began their striptease show for the remainder of the crowd that stared in awe. The smiles

that embraced the faces of these men were unexplain-
able! I could tell that most of them didn't have the opportunity but once in a blue moon, to enjoy such a
time, due to their marriage commitments. So they were
there to party hard until it was over, said, and done.

"Crème is in the house!—Crème is in the house!—
Crème is in the house!"

"Roof! Roof!" the crowd began to Q Dog bark as
they chanted, "Crème is in the house!"

Diamond turned her nose up as the majority of the
room gave praises to Crème. "What the fuck? Crème is
in the house," she said in disbelief.

Suga was right behind her when she exclaimed what
the fellas were yelling. He lowered his head toward her
ear and said softly, "Fuck Crème, you're the tightest in
this muthafucka tonight!"

"Thank you, baby." She laid her head back on his
shoulder, making sure her more passionate grind excited him. The crowd didn't give a fuck about her feelings as they hovered over Crème's seductive, floor grinding dance. Fingers danced wildly, exploring the likes of
Crème, and likewise, Diamond. Dollars graced the
waistline of the two ladies. Lap dances excited the
men, and drinks were consumed.

"Where is Karmel?" Suga's brother, Malik, yelled.
He had made it in from out of town to celebrate his
family with the others.

"Where that other girl?" he asked again.

"Who in the fuck wanna know?" she asked. Karmel
stood confident with all eyes on her! She had on her
tiger-skin bodysuit and high heels to boot.

"Where the fuck is Suga? Betta yet, who the fuck is
Suga?" she asked. The crowd, as a team, began to ooh
and ahh, on key!

"Are you Suga?"

"Yes, love, I am," Suga replied.

Karmel reached into Suga's sweat pants, grabbing hold of his penis. "How sweet is this, Suga?"

"I hope you're not a diabetic!" Suga smiled.

Karmel smiled an innocent but seductive, schoolgirl smile, pleased by what she heard and held with her clutch. She pulled him closer and ran her lips along the sides of his neck, nibbling softly on his earlobe. "I wanna taste the sweetness of this, Suga!"

Midnight pulled a chair up to Suga and Karmel sat him down, climbed on top, and rode him. Both of her hands rested on the back of his neck as his head rested in between her breasts.

"If you won't suck 'em, I will," Midnight yelled. He pulled one of her breasts to meet his lips.

"Come on, baby." She led Suga to the hot tub. Suga was already prepared. His brother had told him to wear swim trunks. He stripped down to just his swim trunks, and the crowd chanted, "Yeah!"

Diamond began to enter the water; the bubble bath was about to be poured.

"Wait." Diamond grabbed the bubble bath. "What kind is this?"

"It is bubble bath!" Malik said.

"I'm sensitive; I can't use just any ole kind in my water, it will irritate me," she said sweetly.

"Okay, honey, but this shit right here is all natural," Malik said.

Karmel warranting Diamond's attention, said, "Baby, I will take care of this right here if you're not comfortable . . . okay?" Diamond agreed and continued to entertain the crowd with Crème, as everyone who wasn't busy with other things, watched the hot tub!

## Suga
## (Hot Tub)

"Dayuuum! My phone keeps ringing off the hook!" Suga looked at the caller ID to see who was calling?

"Hello? Yo, dog, what's up?" he said, excited that his brother Malik was calling.

"Malik, what are you doing here in Tampa?" Suga asked.

"I came up here on business and I need to see a man about a Hennessy mule. I need you here at my hotel by 9 PM. And wear swimming trunks under your clothes."

"Wear swimming trunks?" Suga asked, confused.

"Yeah, nugka, swim trunks! And be at the Airport Hilton at 9 PM."

"Nine?"

"Yeah, nine! Are you deaf?"

We both chuckled. It was kind of silly of me to have him repeat what I know I heard him say, loud and clear.

"A'ight, brother. Later."

It was going on 5 PM already. I had tons of things to do and my main man, Brian, was flying in from Detroit in less than an hour. Road rage was developing from these knuckle-headed drivers, holding up traffic while rubbernecking. I honked the horn and yelled from my window. "Stop rubbernecking, ASSHOLE!"

"Eat a dick, nugka!" is what was insultingly, yelled back. Man, if I had had more time, I would have picked a fight with that punk-ass fool, but I didn't; so I took my bump and rode on into the setting of the sunset.

Brian's flight was on time. We greeted each other with a hug and we caught up on old times, while we drove around running errands.

The running around made us hungry, so we stopped at the local Chinese spot for some grub. There, is where I met Lisa. She was just the right height, but the wrong complexion. She had the right body but the wrong hair do. On a scale of one– to ten, she was a five, so I had no choice but to pass. I kicked a little conversation, got the digits and passed them to Brian. Hopefully, he would be able to get some ass before he returned to the big "D."

She had an attitude like she was hot; I guess folks had been gassing her up, filling her head full of that bull. She pushed a nice little purple compact car with mirror tint on the windows, and her license plate read NEX-LVL. Umph! I wanted to know what that meant. As she drove away, I looked at Brian looking at the number he held in his hand.

It was getting close to nine-thirty, and I was supposed to have met with Malik at nine. Shit! We floated by the house to change and to drop Brian's luggage. I scrambled to find my trunks. Shucks, I haven't worn those things in almost a year, but alas, they were found and we could be on our way.

I called to tell Malik I was on the way, and as usual, he yelled, "Hurry up, nugka. I've been waiting on yo ass for about an hour already!"

"I'm on my way up there now, punk. Chill out!"

"Are you there? Can you hear me?"

"Yeah," I said into my receiver.

"Good!"

*Click!* He hung up the phone.

"Punk!" I exclaimed.

"Hey, man, stop at a store. I want to grab a beer," Brian asked.

"Not a problem, there's a store right there," I pointed.

"Do you want one?" Brian asked.

"Yeah, grab me one and make sure it is cold," I yelled before the car door shut.

Brian returned to the car with a six-pack of beer. "Oh snap! Turn that up, dog. That is my shit!" he said before taking his seat.

The hotel was around the corner from where we were.

"You have a call from . . .!" my cell notified me.

"Hello," I answered.

"Where you at, dog?" It was Malik.

"I am in the parking lot."

"Well, get your ass up here then!" Malik barked.

"Come on, Brian. Malik is rushing me to come up to his room."

"Malik's here?" Brain asked.

"Yeah. He's here to see a mule," I offered.

"A mule?" Brian was puzzled.

Malik opened the door into a world like no other. I could smell the chronic and the alcohol as their scents escaped into the hallway; I could hear the cheers as we strolled in. As soon as I entered the room, some fine-ass honey approached, then another! *Dayuuum* was the only thing going through my head. Each one of them was rubbing a part of their body on me, and I was enjoying every minute of it. A smile graced the handsomeness of my face. I felt like a pimp in a Ho Store.

"Hi, I am Diamond," she said.

I thought to myself, *You sure are. And in the rough too!* She was thicker than a bowl of cold grits! She had the smile of an angel and an ass like a horse. She definitely was a thoroughbred. One cent short of a dime on a scale of one– to nine!

"Hey, what's the occasion?" I asked.

"Tonight we are celebrating Suga!" Midnight said. "And the next party will be for me, for being the blackest nugka in the room!"

Everyone laughed at my best friend's silliness.

We embraced, and Midnight whispered, "Enjoy," in my ear; then burst out with, "Now pour that man a glass of Hennessy with a splash of his favorite!"

He was sippin' Hypnotic and it seemed to have already taken effect.

I grabbed Diamond on her ass and pulled her to me, winding my waist, sipping my drink, while stroking it gently until my dick was rock hard!

Diamond reached back and squeezed my ass, pulling me in closer, intensifying our gyration. Soft moans grew stronger as she simulated a climax.

"Fuck me, Suga! Fuck me!" she was saying softly in my ear. "Oh yeah, daddy! I like that. Do that shit! Fuck that ass!"

My gyration turn into a pumping motion; my lips disappeared with concentration. I was determined to let her know what I was working with. Even the presence of Crème couldn't distract me from what I had already set my mind to.

Crème approached me from behind, sandwiching me between her and Diamond. She reached around and grabbed my stiffened penis; she rubbed it and stroked it through my sweat pants. Crème tucked her bottom lip in. By the look on her face, she was pleased with what she held in her hand.

Midnight grabbed a handful of Crème's ass. She turned around and he put her breast between his big moistened lips. She screamed in ecstasy, with one hand cupping the back of his head, bringing him forth to enjoy a mouthful of her beauty.

"It's a party!" Midnight yelled.

"Crème is in the house!—Crème is in the house!" the fellas had begun to chant.

"Crème is in the house?" Diamond said, not believing what the crowd was yelling as they all watched her.

I knew she was feeling unappreciated and I had to tell her the truth; so I leaned toward her ear and told her she was the tightest bitch in this muthafucka tonight!

She said, "Thank you, baby," as she laid her head on my shoulder.

By this time, another fine-ass honey came from the back. She was wearing a tiger-skin body suit.

"Where the fuck is Suga? Betta yet, who the fuck is Suga?" she said.

Everyone began to ooh and ahh on key.

"Are you Suga?"

"Yes, love, I am," I replied.

She reached into my pants and grabbed hold of my penis. "How sweet is *this,* Suga?"

"I hope you're not a diabetic!" I smiled.

She smiled an innocent but seductive, schoolgirl smile. Pleased from what I had said to her and from what she held in her hand, she pulled me closer and ran her lips along the sides of my neck, nibbling softly on my earlobe.

"I wanna taste the sweetness of this, Suga!" she said, as she gestured with my pecker in hand.

It felt so sensuous and sexy that I exhaled.

My dick was so hard I thought I was gonna cum right there on the spot! A premature ejaculation is not cool. I fought not to feel intimidated by the woman and I struggled not to feel embarrassed by all the homies watching.

A chair was pulled up to my ass and before I knew it, she had sat me down, climbed on top and was riding me like a cowgirl in a rodeo. Both of her hands rested on the back of my neck, and my head rested between her breasts.

Midnight yelled, "If you won't suck 'em, I will!" He pulled one of her breasts to meet his lips.

"Come on, baby." She led me to the hot tub.

*This is why he told me to wear trunks,* I thought. I was glad my brother told me to wear them.

Stripping down to just my swim trunks, I heard the crowd shout, "Yeah!"

Diamond began to enter the water; the bubble bath was about to be poured.

"Wait!" Diamond grabbed the bubble bath. "What kind is this?"

"It is bubble bath!" Malik said.

"I'm sensitive; I can't use just any ole kind in my water. It will irritate me!" she said sweetly.

"Okay, honey. But this shit right here is all natural," Malik said.

Karmel directed all of Diamond's attention toward her and said, "Baby, I will take care of this right here (pointing at me) if you're not comfortable . . . okay?" Diamond agreed and got out of the tub.

I was like, *Shit!* I thought I was gonna have two at once.

Diamond began to entertain the fellas with Crème, while everyone else who wasn't busy with them, watched Karmel and I in the hot tub!

The water was warm as I waited for the treat at hand. Karmel began to ride upon my shaft, moaning softly. "Take this off!" she whispered in my ear.

I discreetly removed my trunks. Since my hands were already beneath the suds rubbing gently on Karmel's ass, no one saw them come off. I tucked them firmly underneath my ass cheeks, so they wouldn't float to the top of the water. My brother, with his slick ass, slid me a condom—it was a Magnum! I looked at him like, *nugka, I don't have a big dick. This shit might slip off.*

He returned a look as if to say, *Well.*

Even when we were younger and I had to borrow contraceptives from him, he'd give me a Magnum. Even then I asked, "Why did you give me this big-dick condom? You know my shit ain't that big!" He just laughed.

I slid the big-dick condom on, anyway. I'd rather try and protect myself, than to not to wear any protection at all. It was safer for the both of us, anyway.

She reached within the waves of the water and inserted me inside of her, breaking the matrix of her vaginal walls. Suddenly, the warmth of her covering me initiated a spark of passion within me. I searched for that perfect angle with every lustful thrust of my penis. She moved up and down, finding her rhythm, finding herself enjoying this good dick being administered to her.

Karmel was giving me a therapeutic massage like no other. Her medicine was curing me of all troubles, healing me of past pains, and nourishing me with juices that were all natural!

My hands rampaged along her smooth skin, squeezing gently here and there, caressing where necessary, causing her to moan in ecstasy—moan in lust—squeezing back, giving more of herself than expected. I am sure there was a chemistry there, hidden somewhere beneath the sins we were committing. Escaping through our touch grew a new relationship. I almost made love to this stranger the way I would my lady, with just a touch away from a meaning.

She moaned again. This time, feeling that feeling that she was feeling, her breathe began to speak of orgasmic pleasures. She jerked inconsistently before pulling my naked frame from the waters, leading me to the bed to finish all of what we had started.

Many of the fellas had left once the first group of moans had begun. Only a few of us were left to close the night: Malik, Brian, Crème, Diamond, and a friend of Malik's named Kelvin.

Soaked with water and sweat, I laid beneath her sexiness . . . once again she rode Mr. Good Dick. I began to find my new rhythm, and with confidence, I began to gyrate, penetrating her with accuracy, trying to hit that G-spot. She and I raced toward the finish line of our current event, and she won. Right in mid-stroke and in the midst of turning that sweet ass over to another pleasure-filled position, she dismounted and disappeared into the bathroom.

I pulled the covers over my stiffened dick; surprisingly, the condom was still attached to my pecker.

*Damn! Maybe my dick is big enough for Magnums?* I thought.

Crème climbed her sexy ass on top of me and began to play friskily, teasing my every emotion. With hands touching every inch of her body, leading her to climb on next, I invited her to feel me. After not being fully satisfied, and lying naked with an empty condom, I was one second from yanking that condom off and fucking Crème' raw dog! She simulated pleasure by moaning and quickening her pace upon my dick.

I tried with every emotion my body had left within to signal to her that I was ready and willing to get it on! "Come on, baby."

*Smack! Smack! Smack!*

My attention was drawn to this intimidating figure which stood hovering above me.

*Smack! Smack! Smack!*

"Malik!! Put that thing away!" My brother stood over me, smacking Crème on the ass with his naked dick.

Karmel must have signaled Crème, because in a flash she and the others were dressed and heading out of the door. I looked at my watch; it was 3:10 AM and I was still willing to party.

Not wanting to go to sleep, I called Midnight and asked what he was in to. To make a long story short, I ended up in the shower jerking off to the trickle of warm water. Once I got my release, just like any man, I curled up in bed and fell fast asleep, until wakened by the morning sun.

That day, I felt cheated that I hadn't gotten my rock off with Karmel. And now I feel like she owes me at least one more opportunity to finish what we started in the Hot Tub.

*Rory Leon*

## Married Men Can't Do!

She was a fan of my writings. I found myself attracted to her because of her feminine ways. Her looks are astonishing. People would tease us saying we looked like we were brother and sister. She has thin lips, high cheeks bones, and a brown complexion, all of which were similar to my features.

Our smiles danced wildly when we talked to each other. Our conversation seemed to flow with ease. She seems as if she could be my perfect soul mate, but I don't really believe in that soul mate stuff. If there was such a thing, I believe that only percentages lower than 10 percent of the world's population, ever finds their soul mate.

I believe in lust, opposites attract, and acting upon instinct. I wanted to know what she felt about this, so I pondered with thoughts of how I would get it across that I needed to know how she felt. Umm! I know. I will write her a story!

She told me I was cool. And once before she told me that a married man couldn't do anything for her. I beg to differ! There is so much I could do for her; there is so much I can show her. However, by her statement, it would have been more appropriate for her to say, "I am not ready for a man like you."

I thought of how I would treat her, love her, and show her the many ways I could prove to her that she was wrong about married men. Her beauty floored me. I mean in many aspects, she is perfect. I didn't know her that well, but I was willing to learn. I wanted to be in her world, if only for a brief moment, if only for one night. Dayuuum, I'm starting to sound a bit like Luther Vandross.

I watched the sweet swagger of her walk as she approached. Her athletic appearance made me want to workout. Fitness is the in-thing now, and maybe I should try it . . . Sheiit, I am not a fool.

"Hi, Anthony Paul Michaels."

Why do women insist on calling a brotha by his whole name? Can I get an Ant? Or maybe Tony!

"Hi, love, how are you doing?" I replied after fussing.

"Fine," she spoke softly.

Damn! There goes that sweet-ass feminine stuff again. Sounding all sexy, like she's hinting at something. Man, she followed it with a smile!

I began to feel as if we were gonna end up getting into one another before our friendship ended. She is very attractive and I am attracted to her. Might I add that curiosity has my number!

We conversed for a bit, exchanging smiles and laughter, even a couple gazes between words. I wanted to kiss her lips, seeking their softness; I wanted her to feel the passion behind mine. I wanted to feel her small waist embracing my hands as I draw nearer. She leaned into me slightly and closed her eyes; I did the same. Our lips touched . . .

"What is your opinion on that?" she asked, taking me out of my daydream.

"Excuse me. I am sorry. I didn't catch all of that. Would you repeat it?" I stated, licking my lips, hoping she didn't notice me staring at hers while she talked.

I couldn't concentrate, knowing I wanted her. I know if I was to have a single chance to show her me, it would be phenomenal—an experience she and I would forever share in our hearts. We talked a while longer before saying our good-byes.

"I like you," she said; then she touched my face softly with the palm of her hand. I kissed it.

"Thank you," I said.

With a smile she turned and walked away. In my mind I was saying, *Walk slowly, so I can watch.* My eyes lustfully played with the idea of having the opportunity to satisfy this young and vibrant ebony queen.

A week had managed to escape us. I was sitting in my truck when she entered the parking garage. She got out of her Mazda wearing spandex and a T-shirt, looking as if she had just come from working out. She appeared very energetic and she had qualities that kept men lusting for her; although, working out had robbed a good portion of her ass! Besides, she would need to workout to keep up with the likes of me!

A boyish grin came upon my face.

She waved, her mouth motioned, "Good morning, Anthony Paul Michaels."

I gestured for her to wait briefly, so we could walk into the building together and share a small conversation. She did.

I opened the door of my truck before removing the key from the ignition. I wanted her to hear the song I was playing: "Say Yes" by Floetry.

. . . *All you gotta do is say, yes!* I began singing.

She smiled. "Good morning, love."

"Good Morning," I said, returning her greeting.

I slowed my pace, placing myself slightly behind her, my eyes taking in all of what she has to offer; enabling her to turn a quarter-inch while she talked.

## Kubuki Love

"What song was that?" she asked as if she hadn't heard it played before.

"'Say Yes' by Floetry."

"Is that new?"

"Yeah . . . Do you have a favorite song?"

"No. Not really."

"You sound like a white girl!"

"What?"

"Yes. You sound like a white girl when you talk."

"Unh-uh, boy, no, I don't. You're so silly! Why do you say that?"

"I dunno. You just do."

"Why do brotha's think when a sista speaks with proper English, she sounds white? You don't want a sista that's educated? You want them to be ignorant and blind to the social surroundings, causing them to depend on you sorry ass brothas? Maybe you want them slow, slightly behind the educational curve?

"You know, more of you brothas need to speak with proper English or a little bit of intelligence, instead of slicing and dicing the English language."

*Whoa, what just happened?* I thought. I see where this is going. I quickly changed the subject, trying to calm the conversation.

"You promised to come by the office. Are you ducking me? A broken promise is the same as a promise not kept! You'll make it up to me. Also, I am not e-mailing you anymore."

"FYI: I had to do the schedule for Sunday. I'm a very busy person. And no, I'm not ducking you. You can come to my office. I don't bite. I will not make a promise again. I'll just show up when I can!" she said; then we went our separate ways.

Damn! What just happened? And maybe I wanted her to bite. Biting is not such a bad thing! I think maybe I should wait a while before I do talk to her again. At least until things calm down a bit. I was feeling like I hit a sore spot with her that would adversely affect our friendship. I wasn't sure if she was mad with me or just firmly stating a point.

We haven't spoken since . . .

I was holding to what I'd said. I wasn't e-mailing her again. I'm not e-mailing someone that can't even reply with a word or two to say, I am busy now, so I will e-mail later. I know she's a busy person, but shit, it ain't like my job is a walk in the park! Damn. How can I get to speak with her again? I asked myself plenty more questions before reaching a solution. Maybe I'll jot something down on paper and hand it to her. A poem or a story—a poem and a story about us and how I feel! Maybe even a formal apology.

So I did just that, putting my heart and soul into a sublime piece: words that would trace the outline of my passion for her. A moment my heart can become real with her.

So I wrote **YOU!**

## YOU!

I enjoy your presence like kids enjoy candy.
Like a well-kept secret
Or a scent of a rose!
My smile dances with your smile for a while!
During walks and talks
Let me be your best-kept secret that no one knows.
Use my mind for your advantages,
Use my body for whatever!

### *Kubuki Love*

Embrace what could be,
And let that last forever!
You're as sweet as fruit,
Because your sweetness comes naturally.
Sharing with me . . . YOU! would be mentally and physically nourishing!
So cup your hand to cover my ear,
And whisper something's that means nothing.
Watch my smile for a while that dances with you lustfully.
My eyes shut to fathom the thoughts of you next to me.
No sex!
Just yet!
Just you and I cuddling.
Soft music escapes as if you were romancing . . .
The thoughts of you and I lustfully dancing.
If you knew
What this married man could do,
Loving me would never be a mistake!
Caress my voice in these words and keep this as a personal keepsake.

**Shooz**

**Sista . . .**

I can't believe the nerve of him, saying I sound like a white girl! I don't care if he doesn't e-mail me. "He needs to worry about e-mailing his wife!" I mumbled under my breath in a huff.

At my desk, I energized my personal computer and the radio, which sat in the corner of my desk next to a picture of my sister.

. . . *All you gotta do is say, yes!*

39

I turned my attention to the song playing. The song was sinking its way into my soul. It began ripping through the matrix of my heart, causing me to think of how silly we had just acted. His face appeared, singing the song.

The words played over and over again in my head. It must have been written for me. Whitney Houston said it correctly in the movie *Waiting to Exhale* when she commented on love songs and who wrote them, for whatever reason.

It dawned on me how I spat relationship-threatening words that could cut like knives, and then I chuckled. It wasn't funny. I just felt silly for the way I over re-acted. He must think I am a nut case.

My left hand covered my girlish grin and I chuckled again. Oh my God, I was feeling real silly about now. A tear raced along my cheek. I sniffed while wiping it away.

*Open up your mind and just rest. I'm about to let you know you make me so,* the song continued. My heart began to release a piece of me to him. He is handsome and his personality is inviting.

*Why do all the good guys get scooped up quickly, and us single women are left with dogs and homosexuals?* were my thoughts. His smile excites me. His eyes deeply hold a story left to be told. Damn, what if?

The song stuck in my head the remainder of my workday. When I got home, I downloaded it onto my laptop, then played it repeatedly until I fell asleep.

"Who could that be knocking at my door?"

"Hello, are you Sista?"

"Yes," I said to the gentleman on the other side of the door.

## Kubuki Love

"Ma'am, this car is for you." He gestured toward the limo waiting curbside. The chauffeur opened the door for me. I could see the legs of a gentleman wearing a suit. The driver helped me inside the limo. I smiled when I saw that the gentleman was Anthony Paul Michaels.

"Good evening, love," he said in his sexy voice with those sensuous lips. He poured us a Daiquiri; it was virgin because he is a non-drinker. He reached over and turned the volume up on the CD player. KEM was playing. We were talking over the soothing sounds for what nearly seemed an hour.

The driver slowed to a stop, then he got out and opened the door. "Ma'am." He extended his hand to receive mine, offering help to exit the vehicle. We were at the Blue Shooz Restaurant, one of Virginia Beach's finest rhythm and blue spots. We were seated by the window that overlooked the ocean. The table setting was elegant and complemented by forget-me-nots. A card was attached that read: I APOLOGIZE.

We enjoyed dinner and a little dancing. A live band was playing this night. We talked gently, staring in each other's eyes. I forgot for the moment he was a married man with a family. I became lost in the moment and he had been the perfect gentleman the whole evening. I leaned toward him. We kissed. I had never experienced a man like him before. I placed my hand behind his head and my tongue lodged into his throat. He placed his hands inappropriately on my ass! We stopped and collected ourselves.

On the drive home we drank from sin's cup! Kissing! Touching! Wanting each other. I felt adventurous. I invited him in for some tea—and me. I had never done anything like this before. He was my first. Being

forward with a man was a new thing for me. I undressed him with my eyes, then with my hands. His
chest felt so good! His nipples hardened as I teased
them with my tongue.

Without a second more of hesitation, I took him into my mouth, giving him the warmth of my soul, the
burst of passion from within me. I didn't just suck his
dick, I made love to it. I closed my eyes and got into
what I was administering to him. It felt so real to me
that I moaned. I became moist. My walls began to ache
for his hardness. His dick was the perfect size. It wasn't
too big, and by far, wasn't small! I wanted him to penetrate these sweet walls of mine, sending me into a vibrant series of jerks. He began gyrating slowly. Moans
escaped his lips. I didn't want him to cum in my mouth,
so I stopped.

His dick looked like a banana with two cherries
stuck in it. He picked me up into the straddle position
and carried me over to the bed. His large hands moved
smartly about my breasts. His sexy lips kissed my skin
softly. He circled areas with his tongue that caused me
to flinch playfully. I put my hand on his head to stop
him, but didn't because it began to feel so good. I
moaned, we moaned.

He circled around the mountain with his tongue,
the same as he did other skinned areas. Lapping up
juices emitted from my nectar seemed to be a delicacy
to him. We moaned together, again.

"Anthony! Ooh shit! Anthony, baby!" I exclaimed.
Damn! He was licking and sucking. And he even put
his chin into it!! I squirmed about. "I'm gonna cum.
Ooh, GOD! Ooooooh, oooooooh, baby, you feel so good."

"Anthony!" I yelled.

### Kubuki Love

My eyes shut tighter than a nat's ass! The trembling sensation caused my legs to close, leaving me in the fetal position. I opened my eyes to find a puddle in my panties. I had my first wet dream.

The next morning at work I spoke with him. I told him how I never meant to neglect him. He gave me a story of us, and made me a poem. My heart melted. The poem was sweet. I especially liked the part about me being naturally sweet like fruit. We spoke with smiles that lasted a while and danced with each other lustfully. I still hold a story untold of him sexually sexing me!

## NAG

"Damn! What does this bitch want?" I exclaimed during my walk inside Farm Fresh super market. My eyes frowned upon the caller ID displaying DON'T ANSWER on my cell phone.

"Hello?" I answered.

"Whatcha doing?" she asked.

"Nothin'," I stated just as plain as I could.

"Are you busy?" she asked.

"Always," I replied.

"Want me to call you back or can you talk?" she wanted to know.

"Wassup?" I asked, trying to get to the point.

"Nothin'. Wassup with you?" she asked.

"Nothin'. Why?" I began gathering an attitude.

"Can I see you tonight?" she asked.

"Damn," I said to myself, looking at my sons who were cruisin' the store with me. Silence fell upon our conversation.

"Are you there?" she questioned.

"Yeah," I replied.

"Did you hear me?" she asked.

"Yeah," I replied again.

"Do you have an answer?" she asked.

"Yeah," I replied, yet again.

I thought the one-word answers would tell her something, but it didn't! She has called me every day this week now and at least five damns times a day, asking me the same shit.

"Well, are you gonna tell me what it is?" she insisted.

"Maybe," I said.

"Maybe?" she questioned.

"Yeah!" I snapped.

"Maybe what?" she asked.

"Maybe. But it depends on how you're gonna react," I explained.

"So you're saying no?" she asked.

"No, I didn't say that. You're putting words in my mouth," I told her.

"So, why don't you just tell me?" she demanded, then waited for my answer.

"I'm watching my boys tonight and I'm not sure I have enough time for what you want," I explained.

"How do you know what I want?" she asked.

I smacked my lips loudly into the phone. "I know what you want," I stated.

"So, why don't you come give it to me?" she asked.

"I told you I'm babysitting," I replied.

"Well, how about I come around there and pick you up, and we ride up the street?" she asked.

"NO!" I yelled.

"Why not?" she inquired.

"I told your ass before. I can't let you know where my girl lives," I said.

"If I was your friend you would," she said.

"If you were my friend, you would not ask me to do that!" I replied.

"I am your friend," she said.

"Oh yeah!" I said.

"Yeah," she confirmed.

"I don't feel much like fuckin', anyway. After you give me sweet kisses below, I'd be ready to go," I explained.

"Oh, is that all you want?" she said nastily.

"No . . ., but if you were my friend, you would understand. I guess your friendship isn't as loyal as you say it is, is it?" I asked.

"You just want me to suck your dick?" she asked.

"That's what friends are for!" I said.

I smiled, knowing that she would be pissed and not call me for a while, accusing me of bruising our relationship and her feelings. But I didn't give two fucks what she felt. The sound of her irked me so bad that I programmed "don't answer" in my cell, which displayed when she called from home, and "nag" when she dialed from work. She got slick on me one time. The bitch went and bought a cell phone. For a while, no information would display when she called.

"Come over then!" she said.

My mouth flew wide open waiting for my foot; nevertheless, I had to play it cool because she had just pulled my card. It was my play now and I knew I couldn't fuck it up.

"I will see you in thirty minutes. I have to get the boys in bed," I assured her.

She had me at my weakest point. I got the boys some milk and cereal; I grabbed tomorrow's dinner and headed home. After I got the boys in bed, I told them that I had to make a quick run back to the store, and for them to go to sleep. They are old enough to understand, being thirteen and eleven. They were responsible enough to be left alone for twenty minutes. I hurried out the house in loose shorts and a wifebeater— no underwear for easy access. I called her to let her know I was on the way.

She lived less than five minutes away. I darted up and through a few side streets, until I reached her apartment. The lights were out. The TV provided a dim illumination from the back room. I knocked softly on the door two times, so she could answer. She knew I would be there within minutes of me calling her. The door opened and there she stood in a T-shirt and shorts, with one crutch under her right arm.

"Come in. How are you?" she asked.

"A'ight, and you?" I asked politely.

"I'm fine," she stated, then closed the door behind me and managed to hobble in tow. "Can I have a hug and kiss?" she added.

Man, I was ready to get the fuck out of there before her meter went off. But I decided that I'd made it this far, so I gave her a hug and a kiss like she was one of my parents, and not one of my fuck partners. I managed to let her know by doing that, that this was not what I came here for. Sensing my uneasiness, she eased me down on her couch. My dick had already begun hardening like Bondo when she pulled my shorts off. While on her knees, she began to massage my thighs, working her way toward the bulk of it all.

It didn't take much for me to stand stronger than the Million-Man March. With her hand, she gently squeezed my dick, holding it like she was hitchhiking—her thumb parallel with my shaft. As she stroked, some juices appeared on the tip of my shaft. With her thumb, and the skin of my dick pulled to the tip like it was a turtleneck, she circled the wetness covering the head of my dick. My shit looked like a licked Milk Dud! After she glazed it up, she took it to the head like a champ! Stroking and sucking me until all I could do was lay my head back on the couch, and let her work.

"Aw, yes!" I moaned.

I tightened my penal muscle when I was coherent enough to hear the slurping noises, similar to the ones I made when eating a Bomb Pop.

"Mmmmm!" she moaned.

My eyes rolled into the back of my head. My lips looked as if I was blowing out smoke.

"Mmmmm!" she slurped.

It was feeling so damn good, I wasn't about to let another moment escape without me looking at what she was doing. I elevated my head just enough to look at her go down like a "professional dick sucker." Her thick, pink tongue was licking my dick like she was trying to catch melted ice cream running down a waffle cone.

"Shit!" The sensation was beginning to get the best of me. I didn't want it to end so quickly. I smacked her hand, which aided this fine pleasure, and said, "Stop cheating and finish eating."

With no hands, she bobbed up and down displaying true skills. I tried to blow a hole in the back of her neck when I came. When I looked down, she had a grip on my dick. I could have sworn it was a forty in a brown bag, and she was trying to get the last drop. With her head tilted back like she was gurgling, she left and went to the bathroom, to spit out my babies and wipe up.

She came back in the room, pointed at the door and told me, "Get the fuck out."

Shit! I ain't no fool—I left. She called continuously the very next day, until I answered my phone. She wanted some dick, and she spoke like I owed her something. I declined 'cause I don't owe her naggin'-ass shit. I made my deposit and the bank is closed.

Fuck that naggin'-ass bitch!

## Paoleria Marie

"Would you like to come up for a drink?" I asked.

"Sorry, love, I don't drink. However, I had a wonderful time and I will come up for a softer beverage, if you have one?" he explained.

"Sure." I smiled at him, then led him up the stairs toward my downtown loft, which overlooked the river.

I couldn't believe this man was extraordinary, and he stimulated my mind as well as other parts of me.

He was slightly older than me; but that is what made him so attractive. His eyes are so deep and he is gentle. I am curious if he can put it down like he says he can.

I returned with soft drinks for the both of us because it's rude to drink while with someone who doesn't drink. I thought it would be a chore to find a man like Tim! I have to have him tonight. I know that I want a relationship. And to have kids one day, I need the love of a man that will bring me flowers, without me asking. I desire a communication between the both us, with no gap.

I have dated men before and all they wanted was the ass! I was happy as hell to be treated like a woman, a lady, and a friend!

Without hesitation!

Without having to ask!

This was a first for me, and I didn't know the proper way to respond. The only way I knew how to respond was with my body language.

"Would you like to listen to some soft music?" I asked.

"Yes, that will be fine," he said in a soft, shylike voice.

I was about to ask the typical question that ladies asked when they wanted THE DICK! Women usually say, "Excuse me, while I slip into something more comfortable." Naw! That wasn't my style. I went about it a whole different way. I knew what I wanted; I was gonna get me some of him. So, I poked my behind parts in his direction while putting on some Maxwell; then I returned to the sofa and took my place beside him—closer than before. I made sure to brush up against him sensuously.

His lips were thin; he sported a set of gumball size cheeks when he smiled. I leaned in and kissed him on the cheek. I felt scared of what he might have thought. Was he feeling that I might be coming on too strong? Men get scared when women are the aggressors. He smiled and said, "Thank you."

I was thinking for what? But he'd read my mind.

"For—being yourself! I admire a woman who can be herself and can roll with the times of today. Most women feel that men are supposed to do everything in relationships, and that it is whorish for them to come-on to men. I find it to be attractive and a turn on."

I listened to him and it surprised me that he caught on so quickly. And at the same time, it also turned me on. He stood and took my hand; he led me toward the center on the room where we danced. His cologne sent me into a world all its own. He caressed the small of my back as if he were tracing letters. It tickled a little and made me laugh.

Oh no, he didn't spin me around and dip me like we were in a 60's movie! "Whoa!" followed by a cute giggle, was my response to the dip.

He pulled me in closer to him; the distance between us became more personal. I could feel him growing against me. I threw in a slight grinding motion, only to increase this urge I have. He returned my grind with one of his own! We danced and laughed for what seemed to be at least an hour or so; then the phone rang!

"Hello?" I said.

"What's up for tonight, baby?" the caller asked.

"Who is it?" I asked, not giving him a chance to really answer before continuing, "I am sorry for the inconvenience, but you have the wrong number. Thank you for calling!" I said and quickly hung up the phone.

It was an old boyfriend of mine trying to make a booty call, but I didn't want to be bothered while I had company. Besides, he was a tired lay, anyway. I was tired of the little boys; it was time for me to experience a man. A real man!

What I mean by "a real man" is a man that has responsibilities. One who has goals in life other than to sleep with every woman he sees. A man that appreciates me enough to bring me flowers—just because. And finally, a man that knows spending time with his lady is paramount. Now that is what I call a MAN! These younger fellas haven't a clue these days.

I returned to what we were doing—you know, the bump and grind and all, when the doorbell rang!

*Ding-dong! Ding-dong!*

My nipples had just begun to protrude and my hand had slid down across his leg, gently inching my way toward his manhood.

*Ding-dong! Ding-dong!*

"Who is it?" I screamed at the top of my lungs. *That came out so ghetto,* I thought. But whomever it was on the other side of that door was bugging me, and I had

51

every intention of leaving their behind on the other side of that door.

*Ding-dong! Ding-dong!*

"Paoleria! Paoleria!" screams came from the hall.

I released a sigh of disgust as I yanked the door open. It was Tina—my good friend.

She began to tell me about her boyfriend hitting her across the face and locking her out of their apartment.

"Can I stay with you?" she asked.

Her mouth was moving a thousand miles a minute, explaining her drama to me. I just gave her the I-got-company look.

"Ohhhh, girl, who is that handsome man you got on your couch?"

"Nun-yun! Tina, you can stay the night, but you got to go right now and come back later on. You know, give me some time to get acquainted with that handsome man on my couch?"

Tina smiled. "Thank you, girl. I appreciate it. And I will be back so you can tell me everything," she whispered.

I whispered right back with a smile, "I ain't telling you shit!" Tina couldn't hold a secret if her life depended on it.

I closed the door and returned to my company. "I hope there're no more interruptions," I said.

"Yeah, me too," he added.

I stood close to him, my hand upon his chest playing with the three strings of hair he had. We shared our first kiss! It felt as if he was inviting me into his world of desire, seduction, and want.

The music released passion that was bottled up inside of me; it allowed some juices to flow unwilling. I couldn't believe how into it I was getting. I was letting go of emotions that I dared to share with any stranger! But he was no stranger to me this night.

He began to slip my blouse off of my shoulder. My erect nipples, he took into his mouth. I moaned in tune with the slurping sound of him enjoying a mouthful of my flesh. Oh shit! It was feeling so good . . . I was taken by surprise learning how this affected me.

I unbuttoned his slacks and stroked all that he bragged about. Damn! I could feel him stiffen in my palm. Most guys are usually hard right before the intercourse. This was the first time I ever had one get hard by my clutch. It started off small, but by the time it was fully hardened, it was out of my hand!

I took his nipples into my hot mouth. "Ummm!" I lowered my kisses; I played childishly in his navel with my tongue. I could feel his dick pulsating, awaiting my touch, awaiting my kisses. I have given head before, but it seemed a little different with this man. Maybe because he was older, and I felt I should take my time and give him total satisfaction. My motions were sensual. I didn't even use my hands, just straight mouth! I was showing off my skills, and by the looks of it, he wasn't complaining one bit.

The look of enjoyment was about his face. His eyes glared down on me in disbelief. The whole story was told when I noticed he had a handful of my hair, aiding my skills by giving him more. I removed his hand, *'cause I can handle mine,* and then I hit him with my famous Blow-Pop style.

He moaned; his stomach muscles tightened in unison with his ass cheeks. He didn't expect what I did next while his hands rested on his hip—I gave him the cherry popper! Yeah, that buckled his knees before he exploded his load into my hair and on my face. The cherry popper gets the best of them! That's when a man begins to enjoy the sucking of his dick to the point near climax, and just before you think he's going to blow his load, you slightly thump his balls. This procedure is what's known as the cherry popper or the nutcracker!

It seemed as if he had a few tricks up his sleeve, also, once we finally made it to the bedroom. He didn't talk much during sex like most of the guys I have been with. Talking loud with their lips and saying nothing with their hips! It was the other way around in this case. He was holding a conversation with his hips and preaching with his lips.

He asked me to mount him. He had what he called the upside-down pound cake. He was so in control of his movements; he moved my body as he pleased. I think I climaxed at least five times! He traced the outer walls of my kitten as he probed with his throbbing member. I began to move my waist like a dancehall girl. Moans escaped my mouth; my walls began to tumble, my body shivered as if I were cold. I noticed myself in a comfort zone, relaxing without reason.

*Ding-dong! Ding-dong! Ding-dong!*
*Thump! Thump! Thump!*
"Poaleria!"

The knock at the door had shaken me from my sleep.

"Wait a minute! I am coming!"

I tossed on my robe and scratched my head as I headed for the door. "Who is it?"

"Tina!"

"Girl, it is two AM!"

## Kubuki Love

"Are you done with your company?"

That is when I noticed that he had left. No note, no kiss on the forehead, no I will see you later—nothing! I was trying to remember what happened. Tina wouldn't stop with all of the questioning.

"Where did you meet him? How old is he? Does he have a wife?" Tina rapidly fired question after question.

Yadda-yadda-ya, on and on, she was being nosey, but I refused to give up the goods, so I said, "You know where the sheets and blankets are. I will see you in the morning." I closed my door and sank my head into the pillows.

Softly, I rubbed the spot where we both laid naked, and a smile came across my face and a shiver touched my body. My eyes closed for what seemed only five short minutes, before the morning light shined brightly into my window. Shucks! It was 7:30 AM. I had better get a move on it if I was to make it to work on time. I started a pot of coffee and went to retrieve the morning paper. Taped to the door was a single rose and a card that read:

Thank you for a wonderful evening.
Thank you for a smile.
Let's spend today together
Doing something wild.
Time with you is special and
Special are you.
I just love the things you do
When you're doing
What you do!

The smile on my face said it all. I held my heart as I read and a tear formed in the well of my eye. Sometimes it is the simplest things that mean the world. I feel beautiful today and I owe it all to you.

## Rini's Drama

Sye threw the cover back, revealing his naked and chiseled frame. "Fuck this shit, Rini! I am tired of every time I want to have sex with you, you reject me! What's up with that, Rini? Are you fucking someone else?"

"No, Sye! I am not fucking someone else! And why when I am not in the mood, you get an attitude and yell out something stupid like I gots-ta-be fucking someone else?"

"Not in the mood? Rini, when are you ever in the mood? We haven't done anything in nearly a month!"

"And?" Rini said with attitude.

"And! Rini, I am a man and I have needs! It isn't good for me to have SBU—sperm build-up! Look at these nuts, Rini; they are swollen from lack of sex!" Sye grabbed hold of himself and began to jiggle his testicles toward Rini's direction. "I'll be wrong if I drifted outside of our relationship, now wouldn't I?"

"What do you mean 'drifted outside of our relationship'?" Rini asked with attitude, rolling her neck side-to-side. "You cheating, Sye?" Tears formed in the wells of her eyes.

"No, Rini! I have not been cheating! Close to, but not yet have I cheated! I have been wanting you and needing you; yet, every time I make an attempt to be with you, you turn your body or close your legs tighter. When you do things like that, it makes me want to go be with someone else because I feel that you have fallen out of love with me."

Rini's facial expression saddened slightly. "Sye, why is sex such a big deal with you? You never touch me like you used to. You just roll over on top of me and expect me to be intimate with you! Where is the foreplay? Can I get a back massage? Can a sista get her neck kissed?"

"Rini, you ain't no sista! Look here, my balls are swollen! My dick got hard the other day when you cooked fish!"

"Sye, what are you saying? I smell like fish?"

Sye burst into tears from laughter. "No, I am not saying that," he laughed, "I'm just saying, baby, that I need you and want you. I just wanna be with my lady. Besides, it's not good to be backed up. I feel the need to release with you."

Rini cut Sye off, "See, Sye, there you go again, thinking with your dick. Yooza sex fiend!"

"A fiend, Rini—you calling me a fiend?" Sye's voice became high-pitched. "Is that how you see me, Rini? A freak? A pervert? Huh, Rini? Is that all I am to you? You know what, Rini, fuck you with your stank-ass pussy! Oops, baby, I'm sorry that slipped!"

It was too late, Rini's mouth dropped so wide open you could drive a truck through it and not hit a single tooth. She ran into the bathroom in tears. She felt so embarrassed that she ran herself some bath water.

Sye stood outside of the bathroom door thinking about what he'd just said, and how it must have sounded coming out the way it did. Butt-ass naked, he leaned against the door trying to take back the Ginsu-words that sliced Rini's heart.

Rini stood in the mirror with tears in her eyes, mumbling the words Sye had said so insultingly. "Fuck you, Rini, with your stank-ass pussy! Humph! My pussy doesn't stink! I bet Suga wouldn't think this pussy

stank you . . . you—you, pervert!" she cried, with her
sexy smile turned upside down.

The water was kind of hot, but she stepped in anyway. The soapsuds outlined her slender frame, steam
rose from beneath her breast-line, and her nipples
hardened from the brisk air that had flown across her
flesh.

Soaking and sulking until her facecloth found itself
circling the pink of her pussy, she began to get aroused;
she began to feel guilty about how selfish she has been
with the poonanny. The water rushed from her head to
her toes, exposing a luscious set of peanut butter
perky breasts, racing toward the mountain of lust and
erasing itself beneath the sexiness of her sculptured
muff.

Rini stepped out of the tub and dried herself with
Sye's towel, not noticing it was his until she was almost dry.

"I will fix his stank ass!" she said to herself. She
reached for his facecloth, and then she wiped her cat
with it. "Now, stank-ass pussy that," she said vindic-
tively.

Rini nearly jumped out of her towel when she opened
the door to find Sye standing there. She began to wonder
if Sye had heard what she'd said. "Move, Sye!" she said,
pushing him aside.

"Please, Rini baby, let me explain."

"There is nothing to explain, Sye."

"But Rini—I didn't mean what I said! I-I-I apologize!

"You apologize? I can't believe you, Sye." She just
shook her head with disbelief.

"Please, baby, I didn't mean it." Sye removed Rini's
towel, allowing it to fall to the floor, then he eased her

onto the bed softly. "Stop, Sye, let go of me! What are you doing?"

"Rini baby, just lay back and relax."

"I am not about to let you stick your dick in my stank-ass pussy!" she said, not meaning for spit to fly out when she said the P-word.

"I'm not going to stick my dick into your pussy. I'm going to . . ." Sye held her hands on the bed as he lowered his head, kissing, licking, and sucking every inch of her body within reach.

"No, Sye," she softly said.

She was resisting but without force. Her voice became soft and passionate. Sye eased up a little on his grip, but not letting go while his wet and hot mouth began sucking her clitoris. He gyrated his face beneath her love. He fully released his hand and moved her legs to a more accessible position. Rini began to rotate her hips, matching the rhythm of Sye's tongue.

She moaned and clutched a handful of the sheets.

"Sye—I am sorry, baby—ooooh, baby—yessss! Oh yeah, baby, that feels so good." Rini began to rub on her own tits, pinching her nipples and intensifying her passion for him. With every moan, Rini's love began to come down further and further until . . . "Ooooh, baby. Ooooh, yessss!"

Her muscles tightened and she fully extended her arms to hold the fighting mouth of Sye. But his neck muscles were much too strong for her. Sye continued to lick and softly suck her clitoris, moving smartly up and down the rim of her juicy and tasty pussy. A sucking and slurping sound escaped Sye's area of concentration.

"Oh shit! Oh shit! Dayuuum, baby . . . I am about to cum again."

## Kubuki Love

The sucking and slurping sound turned into a sloppy wet one. Sye stood over Rini's exhausted and well-relaxed body with his erect penis.

"Rini, I am leaving you! And you didn't do that well at washing it!"

Rini fell speechless for a good ten seconds. She pulled the covers over her and cried for hours. Even after Sye had gathered his belongings and was long gone, she lay lifeless in search of an answer for his actions, with nothing left for her to do but sleep and rest her pain-infested body. She closed her eyes with every hope that the hurt would go away.

The phone rang six times before she leaned over to get it. "Hello?"

"Hey, girl, whatcha doing?" Melaine asked.

"Shit!" Rini answered.

"Damn, girl, you sound bad. What's da-matta wiff you?" Melaine asked.

"Shit!" Rini said again.

"Umm . . . is that all you're gonna say is shit?" Melaine said.

"I don't feel much like talking to anybody right now, Melaine. Sye just left me!" She began to cry again.

"OOOOH, GIRL. I am there. And you better open the door." Melaine hung up and was in the car in a flash.

Fifteen minutes later, Mel, medium brown skin with a fleece sweat suit, was at the door pounding ghetto style. "Girl, open up, it is Mel!"

The unlocking of the latches was Mel's cue not to bang the door down. The knob twisted and the door cracked itself open. Mel pushed her way through the door to see Rini wrapped in covers with her hair a mess.

"Damn, girl, did he hit you? 'Cause we can go find his ass right now and handle some business!"

Weak and emotionless, Rini managed to squeeze a, "No, Sye didn't hit me," from beneath the covers, then made her way to the couch. "We had an argument."

"About what, girl?"

Rini flopped on the couch and tried to ignore Mel's question.

"Come on, Ree-Ree, talk to me?"

"He tried to get some and I didn't feel like doing it, so I prevented him. So, he yelled he was tired and said I was cheating. I called him a freak. He said my pussy smelled like fish, so I washed it; then he ate it and told me I didn't wash it that well and he was leaving. Now he is gone!" She began to cry more.

"Girl, what? That shit didn't make any sense."

Rini started over again, this time speaking a little slower when she spoke.

"We started arguing because Sye wanted to have sex and I didn't. He asked did I have someone else because he and I haven't made love in a month or so."

"A MONTH! Rini, are you crazy? Do you love Sye?"

"Yeah, I love Sye."

"Then you got to give up the poonanny! In order to keep a man, you have to free a man! And the only way to free a man is to free his mind. And the only way to do that is to fuck him well and feed him good. There is nothing more relaxing to a man than being able to release himself within his woman by covering her. My pastor preaches on that all the time."

"Maybe your pastor is a pervert, too." Rini smacked her lips and twisted her head.

## Kubuki Love

"Be quiet, stupid, and listen to what I am telling you! There is no woman that can tell you about a man better than a man can. When men speak, you ought to listen sometimes. They are not hard to figure out. Men like sex; they like to eat! Men like women that are not loose." Mel held a look on her face that may have implied that Rini was loose, or at one time in her life, wasn't faithful.

Rini's face replied with a surprised look like, *Not me.*

"What does Sye do after you two have sex? Does he go out and run a couple of miles? No. He falls asleep, doesn't he?"

Rini chuckled but replied with a, "Yeah, he does."

"Once a man releases all of the tension, pressure, and in y'all's case, SBU, he is relaxed. And when the body is in a relaxed state, it wants to sleep.

"Okay, Ree-Ree, so far, you were in the wrong because one: you never holdout or ration the poon-poon; two: you never use the poon-poon as a tool or weapon; three: when in doubt, go back to step one and two! Now that you have learned a few of the don'ts, you may proceed. So, what else happened?"

Rini continued. "Sye said the other day when I cooked fish, it made his dick hard. And I took that as if he was saying that my pussy stunk! So, I call him a sex fiend, and that's when he said, 'Fuck you with your stank-ass pussy!' I felt so embarrassed, Mel, that I ran into the bathroom and took a bath. When I came out of the tub, he was waiting at the bathroom door for me.

"He held me on the bed while he performed oral sex on me."

"And, and . . ." Mel sat in suspense waiting for the rest of what had happened.

"And!" Rini said with emphasis. "You know I love oral sex—anytime, anyplace."

Mel finished Rini's sentence. "Yeah, yeah, yeah, I know, and anywhere!"

"As I was saying before I was rudely interrupted. Girl, he was eating the hell out of my pussy. His tongue probed in and around my pussy like a pap smear. Sye's tongue is so thick and long that if he had no arms and no legs, he could still manage to pick his nose!"

"DAYUUUM! Ree-Ree, it was like that?"

"Yessss, girl, like that! He ate this pussy so well, my multiple orgasms culminated."

"DAYUUUM!" Mel covered her mouth; her eyes were extended like they were about to pop! "It's like that?"

Rini continued. "After he was done giving me some good face, he stood up and said he was leaving me. The next thing I know, he was gone."

"Girl, stop it! No, he didn't?" Mel burst into laughter.

"No, he didn't what?" Rini was a bit confused with the street slang Mel was using.

"No, he didn't give you a Tyrone's Diner?"

"What is a Tyrone's Diner?" Rini asked, with the most confusing look upon her face.

"That is when you eat-n-run. Lonnie did Stacy like that, but left with a doggy bag!"

"A doggy bag?"

"Yeah, Lonnie tried the Tyrone's Diner, but Stacy had a STD! Girl, Lonnie's mouth is still fucked up! He beat the shit out of her last week when he got out of the hospital." They both shared a laugh.

"Mel, what happened to all of the good men?"

"Ree-Ree, they're in church!"

*Kubuki Love*

"Church?"

"Yeah! Because if the Lord can't save them, then they are not worth saving. And if the Lord can't keep them, then they are not worth keeping!"

"But, Mel, good men are still hard to find!"

"Yeah, Ree. And a hard man is good to find!"

"This is true, Mel. This is true."

"Come on, girl. Let's go grab a bite to eat—my treat, your choice."

"All right, Mel, I wanna go to O.G.'s. I like their service. Also, their salad is the bomb!"

"Let's go."

"And you're buying drinks, too."

"Okay," Mel replied.

She waited patiently for Rini to get dressed, so they could be on their way to O.G.'s.

## Rini and Suga

### Rini

"Hey, hey—heeey, sweetness, slow down for a minute so I can talk to you!" he said in his soft, sexy voice. You know how guys do when they go into a so-called pimp mode. I stopped walking as he trotted up to me. I just stood there as he pitched his game. "How are you doing?" he asked.

"I was doing good until you stopped me!"

"Whoa, honey, I didn't mean no harm. I just wanna holla at you for a minute. You look good and I wanna know you. Is anything wrong with that?"

"Yeah," I said in a halfway snotty tone. "I got something to do, bye!" Then I walked off. He ran up behind me.

"Wait a minute, love. Just hear me out for two minutes!"

"Okay, you got one minute!"

"One minute?"

"Fifty-nine, fifty-eight, fifty-seven . . ."

"Okay, okay! What is your name?"

"Monica," I lied.

"Monica?" he said in an unconvinced way. "That's cute. You kind of look like a Monica. But I was thinking more like a Misha."

"Forty-five, forty-four, forty-three . . ."

"Will you take my number and at least call me when I got more than thirty-three, thirty-two, thirty-one seconds to talk to you?"

I smiled because I was being rude to the boy. "Yeah, but don't get mad if I don't call!" I snapped.

## Kubuki Love

He was cute and wouldn't take no for an answer. He wrote his number down and smiled the sexiest smile I have ever seen on a man.

"Bye, Monica," he said.

I don't know why I told that boy my name was Monica. I guess it was the first name that popped into my head. I don't necessarily think I look like a Monica, but if he says I do, then that's news to me.

I looked at the little piece of paper he wrote on. My grandmother would always say, "You can tell a lot about a person by the way they write." I had no other choice but to smile, his number was 587-SUGA and he had good penmanship!

There was a group of things that I liked about Suga, but at this particular moment, I wasn't interested in him. Now, make no mistake, I don't consider myself to be picky about men; however, it doesn't really matter what their skin color or race is, except for Mexicans, they're really not my type.

I don't like men fat or too skinny, but if I like them as a person, that will eventually not matter to me. I'm all about the person's eyes. I love everything about them. I would say I'm more attracted to guys with light-brown skin tone or a pair of really pretty gray eyes. And don't mistake that for a white man, because that's pretty common; at least to me, anyways. I like for a man to be taller than me, at least about 5'10" plus. I am short enough without having someone shorter than myself.

Suga meets the height requirement among many other qualities, but he is darker than I like and his eyes are definitely not gray! Suga watched me walk for at least a block. I felt like he was a pervert. After all, he is slightly older than I am.

His eyes were deep and that made me wonder about him. I saw life in his eyes. There, laid beauty beyond this man's weak-ass game; and he interested me. Hmmm, maybe I will call him. I smiled.

The first call:

"Hello?"

"Is Suga home?"

"This is he."

"How are you? This is Monica."

"Hi, Monica. I am surprised that you called."

"Why?"

"You sounded as if you really weren't interested."

"I was having a bad day, that's all. Did your parents name you Suga for real?"

"Yes."

"You mean you have no other first name?"

"No. Suga is it, baby."

"Ummm . . . that's different."

We talked and talked; somehow we got on the subject of sex and how we liked it to be done. "I know you asked me about my fantasy, but to tell you the truth, I don't fantasize about sex. It's really not that big of a deal to me. I know that might be a shock to you, but that's really the way I am and the way I feel about it. I do prefer oral sex any day, any time, any where. So, what's yours?"

"I very much so like oral sex," Suga said. "I love to get it than to give it. I want two women to give me head at the same time! And I want to fuck a midget!"

I burst out into laughter. "A midget?"

"Yes, a midget," he said.

## Kubuki Love

I asked why and he said that was something that he couldn't explain. All he knew was he wanted to have sex with one.

"Not just any ole midget, but one with a nice shape!" he exclaimed.

I couldn't stop my giggles. He had tickled me in a way no other man has before. "I think you are a very interesting person; somewhat of a freak, but still interesting. The fact that you like to express yourself sexually, and your imagination taking you to some fantasyland with midgets; I would say some facts like that make you interesting."

"Well, Monica, what are some of the things you like and don't like about yourself?"

"That is a good question, Suga."

"Girl, I like the way you said that. Say it again."

"Say what?"

"My name like you did—*Suga,*" he said sensuously, in a fake girly voice, followed by laughter.

We then laughed together.

"I didn't say it like that."

"Yes, you did."

"*Suga,*" he repeated again, laughing. "Come on, Monica; say it again for Big Suga."

It was silly, but I did it and we shared another laugh.

"So, what do I like and dislike about myself? What I don't like about myself is maybe the fact that I'm a little too skinny. I would like to gain weight by eating and exercising, but I'm not really motivated to do that. That's something I like about myself also: I'm not too fat, so I guess I'm okay the way I am."

"Hey, Monica, you know what?

"What?"

"I think you are a cool, laid-back kind of person who is somewhat to herself; knows what she likes, and goes after it. You like to keep things on the down low. I would like to build on that, what I feel about you. To me, and I am just speaking from what I see because I don't know you yet, I think you are a very attractive young lady, street smart with a lil HLF side."

"What?"

"Oh, my fault—homey-lover-friend. And what I mean by that is, homey: you appear to be a person that is cool; lover: secretively, you get down for yours, and whatever goes down sexually, is you and that person's thang; friend: a person that one can easily converse with and not about all the bullshit! Am I close?"

"I guess you were fairly close. I'm really down-to-earth and it pretty much sounded like me. That was pretty good if you got all of that by just watching me. But that's only one point of view: yours. I wonder if everyone else sees me the same."

"I am sure everyone does. And yes, you're correct about it being my point of view. I think you should just ask a few people and see what type of response you'll get if you ask them that question?"

"Maybe I will."

Before I knew it, Suga and I had talked for quite some time. It was getting late and I had to be at work early. I hated to end our conversation so soon, but I am sure he would understand. Suga is a warm, nice, sweet person. I chuckled to myself wishing I didn't have to break the news.

Oh shit, I forgot! How am I gonna tell Suga that my name isn't Monica? He is gonna hate me. I'm sure he won't want to talk to me again after that, thinking I am full of games.

## *Kubuki Love*

"Suga! I had a great time talking to you on the phone, but I have to get up real early and make it to work."

"I understand, love, and I had a wonderful time on the phone with you, also," he interjected.

"Before you hang up, Suga, I have to come clean with you! I know I shouldn't have, but I didn't know then what I feel now. Suga . . ."

"Monica, wait—the best way to tell someone something is to just say it. And believe me, no matter what you're about to tell me, I will still be thankful to God that I had at least one opportunity to meet you and speak with. You are a sweet person. Thanks for being my blessing."

I felt a mist form in the wells of my eyes as I formed my lips and told him my name was not Monica. I waited for him to hang up on me after yelling "bitch!!" but he didn't, he just asked one question: "What is your name?"

"Rini. And I'm sorry for leading you on. But as I was saying, I had a bad day. Hopefully, I will talk atcha later. Good night."

"Good night, love. I don't have your number, so I hope that you'll call again."

And then we hung up.

## The Closet

This was one of those days where it wasn't shit to do! There I was, laying my happy ass on the couch playing PS2 . . . the phone rang! It was my man, Doc, on the other end, trying to get me to hang out with him at the arcade. At first I declined. But after some convincing, and him saying that he would treat for the first ten dollars of our game playing, I accepted! Ten bucks for us was really a free night of me kicking his ass in Mortal Kombat.

"I'll take you up on that," I said, happy that there was finally something to get into, and also because I am an arcade junkie! We played about five games of the Mortal Kobat before I retired to my old-school favorites: Ms. Pac Man, Galaxy, and Robotron, which I would spend hours playing.

"Excuse me!" I looked over my shoulder to see who was speaking to me in that sexy, soft voice.

*Dayuuum!! Why doesn't the voice fit the woman?* I thought. She sounded sexy, but to my amazement, she was a big girl. She had to be at least 225 pounds. She was about my height and my complexion; her hair was short, and at first I thought she was a fat boy about to get beat up for trying me!

"Wassup?" I replied.

"How are you doing?" she asked.

"I'm fine."

"I see that! What is your name," she drilled.

"Osallo."

I couldn't believe it. Was she hittin' on me? She began sparking conversation just talking about anything and everything! She asked me questions from where I was from to what was my great-great grandma's maiden name. Then there came the final question; my heart was pounding!

"My name is Teresa. What are you doing tonight?" she asked.

"I dunno?" I replied with this dumb-ass look on my face.

She invited me to her crib. No woman had ever hit on me before tonight.

Doc sat aside laughing at me the whole time. "It's cool, playa, handle your business!" he said. "I will catch up with you later." He chuckled.

We all left going our separate ways. Well, Doc and I went our separate ways. Teresa and I went to her place.

The appearance of the house was a shock! It looked like she hadn't done dishes in months and there were clothes everywhere. The bed wasn't even made! I started to walk away. It smelled like baby milk and mothballs up in that piece. But I couldn't leave; I had to stay. My dick was hungry and it needed feeding!

She didn't even hesitate; she went right to work, rubbing and kissing on me. My dick got hard; I knew then it had to be on. I kept telling myself that she wasn't the one and my bulge was saying the opposite. So I just placed my hands around her wide waist and returned her kisses.

Her tongue was so thick and wet it almost choked me. It felt as if I'd swallowed a leach! I know I wasn't attracted to her, but how could I pass up the chance at satisfying the urge of busting a nut or two?

Her fat fingers journeyed across the bulge in my jeans, caressing it gently. She unzipped my pants without me even realizing it. She was a pro! She went down inside my underwear and grabbed the whole johnson. She led me across the room to the couch by my love muscle. She undressed, revealing her big tits and matching stomach. Her ass looked hail damaged with all those dips. I couldn't even tell if she had hair on her crouch from all of her thickness!

She stroked my johnson and then pulled me toward her rear. I guess my dick was going to be the dent puller! It was awkward. I had to position myself under her ass because it was too big to go through and too wide to go around. It wasn't what I expected, nor was it what I was told it would be.

She reached under and grabbed the shaft of my shit and rubbed the outer walls of her mountain of passion. It felt *so* good I planted my hands firmly on her lumpy-ass cheeks. My bottom lip tucked beneath my teeth and my stroke was found! In and out is all I knew. My pace quickened!

"Slow down, baby! You movin' too fast."

I chanted words I heard on the spice channel.
"Yeah, yeah, you like this dick, don't you?" Saying that to her, made me laugh internally.

With my upper body stiff as a board, I began again rocking inward at a slower pace as she requested. "Does it feel good? Huh?" she asked with a heavy breath.

"UMMM-HMMM!" I couldn't speak. I was speechless. My balls were slapping the tightness of her inner thighs and sweat was escaping the pores of my young flesh. Her screams of joy were bouncing off of walls of this junkie-ass room, as her hands clinched the cushions of the couch. She had no idea!

## Kubuki Love

I felt in charge at the moment. I was king of the coochie! My chest muscles tightened in unison with my ass cheeks, pounding her big ass with force.

"Yeah, Osallo—like that! Like that, baby! Punch a hole in this ass."

"I find that impossible!" I said to myself. "Like that? Huh? Like that? Is this what you want, baby; Osallo's dick to punch holes in your shit?"

I kept with the mighty stroke until the magic stick broke. I mean, I was hugging her ass like she was a big lumpy pillow—steady stroking until I came! I hope she didn't notice the tears I released that ran down her back. She probably thought it was sweat. That pussy was wet and good!!! I cried like a baby!

"What's the matter, O?"

"Nothing!"

"Why are you crying, baby?"

I slipped up and let her know she was my first. She thought it was so cute that it was my first time, and that she was the one to bust my cherry.

The fight wasn't over because Teresa found some kind of turn-on from learning about my virginity. She nurtured my weakness back to its strong youth with her lips. Her mouth was so warm, her tongue was so thick, and her touch was invading my privacy. She lowered her lick. My nuts moved about in a circular motion; her hand played slowly. She went toward my brown eye. She parted my cheeks and went to work! Butt-hole, balls, dick—back and forth from one to the other. She had my mind!

*Damn!* I gripped the fabric beneath me, holding on for dear life. I was pulling it so hard, I could hear it ripping! She moaned as if she was licking an ice cream cone in July.

## I'm In Love with a Stripper

"Where have you been?"

"What? Don't no bitch ask Puck where the fuck he has been."

"Where have you been, Puck?" she asked more demandingly. "Were you at, that stank-ass strip club again?" she asked.

"No, Maw-Maw, I wasn't at the club."

"Yes, yo dumb ass was, 'cause I followed you."

"Dumb ass? You're the dumb ass, Maw-Maw, because you followed the wrong car!" Puck yelled.

"Why you always go to that club, anyways? Aren't I enough for you?"

"Maw-Maw, you are 46 years old . . . and you don't exercise."

"What are you saying, Puck?" Maw-Maw asked.

"Woman, I am not saying anything else 'cause I know I will get you mad if I say what is on my mind. When you gets mad, I gets no nookie!"

"Shut up, Puck! All you think about is sex!"

"Shit, ain't nothing else to think about but money and pussy, all of my bills are paid."

"Typical man! Why don't you get a second job, Puck?"

"I already have a second job!" Puck said.

"What is it?" Maw-Maw asked.

"Puttin' up with yo ass, Maw-Maw!" Puck spat then continued, "Yeah, typical woman! You all are all the same: thinking a man can survive off of pussy once a year—thinking that we married each other for love and not for the sex. That is bullshit, Maw-Maw, and as

soon as a man goes and gets himself a little entertainment, y'all start tripping."

"Puck, everything you can get out there you can
get here at home. You just gotta know how to get it.
And then once you get it, you have to know what to do
with it."

"Oh, is that so, Maw-Maw?"

"Yeah, Puck, that is so! All you want is for me to be
a freak for you! I am not your ho!"

"Then what the fuck did I marry you for?" Puck
asked. "I should have married a ho, then I wouldn't be
having this argument, huh?"

"Oh, you want a ho now, Puck?"

"All I am saying, Maw-Maw, is the first thing you
women cutout of the marriage is the sex! Why don't
you cutout something I can be thankful for, like the
nagging, bitching, and the complaining—oh yeah, the
money spending and TV dinners.

"If I want something good to eat, I have to go to
That's My Dog! Why don't you cook sometimes and
give me some loving without me begging for it all of the
damn time?"

"If it will keep you home, I will do it for you," Maw-
Maw said with misty eyes, and genuine love in her heart.

"Okay, Maw-Maw. Your mouth just wrote a check
your old ass can't cash!" Puck smiled as if he was
hearing the winning lottery numbers, while holding the
winning ticket. "It starts immediately, so that you don't
change your mind," Puck stated.

Puck took his cell phone from his pocket and called
his best friend. "Hey, Paul, I'm not coming!" Then he
hung up the phone.

"First, I want you to fix something for me to eat, and then I want to bathe. After that, it's Mista Nasty time! Have your ass in the bed and ready."

Maw-Maw did just as she had promised. Doing everything Puck had asked of her.

Puck laid into her three times before falling asleep. Maw-Maw felt overworked. She couldn't believe that he still had the sex drive of a young man. She had to use a lubricant halfway through the second go around.

The next morning while Maw-Maw was at work, Puck had a stripper pole with a 3-foot circular stage installed in their bedroom. He also purchased a small smoke machine and disco lights to get the full effect of the new club—Club Maw-Maw. Puck changed all of the lighting in the room to red, green, and blue.

It was time to test the scenery. Puck popped the new T-Pain CD in. It was just like a mini strip club. Puck even had a fully-stocked mini bar and refrigerator. It was on . . . Puck got excited and began simulating smacking the ass of an imaginary dancer.

"Puck's in love with a strip-perrr!" he began singing. "Puck's in love with a strip-perrr! Yes, sir!" he yelled, and then he shut everything off and waited for Maw-Maw to get off work.

Puck picked Maw-Maw up from work and headed straight for their favorite restaurant.

"What's the occasion?" she asked.

"I'm just showing my appreciation, Maw-Maw. We are meant for each other and I now know what we mean to each other."

"Puck, have you been drinking?"

"No, Maw-Maw," Puck quickly replied.

"Umm" was Maw-Maw's reply.

## Kubuki Love

Puck ordered steak and shrimp with a double-shot of Cognac. He ordered Maw-Maw a chicken dish with a strawberry vodka daiquiri.

After dinner, they arrived at the house and Maw-Maw noticed Puck had rose pedals leading toward the bedroom. Her smile spoke volumes to Puck and he knew her heart was embraced by the romance in the room. As she came closer to the bedroom, Puck covered her eyes with his hand and whispered, "I have a surprise for you."

The excitement made her giggle.

Puck led her toward the bathroom where he had a nice warmed Jacuzzi bath waiting for her. (I know you're wondering how the water stayed warm while they were out. They owned a very expensive tub that kept the water in the tub heated to the temperature of when the water was first put into the tub. Okay, now back to the story.)

Puck removed his hands from her eyes to reveal a candle-lit bath with a soft aroma of musk. Soft music bounced from wall to wall.

"Maw-Maw, I love you."

"I love you, too, baby," Maw-Maw shared.

Puck undressed Maw-Maw and helped her into the bath. He washed her from head to toe, and then dried her in the same manner. Maw-Maw was in heaven. Puck hadn't been this romantic to her since they were in their twenties.

Maw-Maw put her silky house robe on and headed toward the room with the most girlish grin he had ever seen.

She motioned for Puck to follow her for another night of passion. She hadn't fully recovered from the night before, but the evening's events had her excited and moistened to the point where that didn't even matter. She opened the bathroom door and entered the room, and her mouth dropped in amazement.

Puck pressed the button on the remote and the club music started. His hands flew in the air and he began winding his waist.

"Awe, Puck-Puck . . . baby, bay-bay!"

The bass bumping; the lights and the smoke, almost spoiled Maw-Maw's mood.

"Puck?" Maw-Maw said.

*Smack!*

Puck smacked her on the ass and then yelled, "Coming to the stage . . . Ta-a-as-tee!"

Maw-Maw giggled and figured what the heck, he'd gone through all this trouble, she might as well play along.

Dancing for her husband made her feel sexy and he marveled at her body. So she began to get into it a little more. Maw-Maw knew a little something!

She began dancing like she had done it before. Puck's eyes grew as he took in the explicit sight. He grabbed a drink from his mini bar, then gulped it down.

"Make it rain on them hoes, I make it rain." He fanned money at Maw-Maw—crisp twenties. "I make it rain, I make it rain," Puck sang.

"Make it bounce, Maw."

"Stop!"

"Now rock wiff it."

"Stop!"

"Now wiggle it! Drop it. Drop it. Drop it like it is hot!"

*Smack!*

"Whooo, wee, Maw-Maw, you got a fatty!"

"Puck, if you slap me on the ass again, I am getting down from here!" Maw-Maw exclaimed. "Matter of fact, no touching the dancer," she reiterated to him.

She continued to excite Puck. She began to see how Puck acts while at the clubs. The more he drank, the more he partied. Puck jumped on stage with Maw-Maw and began getting his strip on.

"Get down, Puck!"

He laughed, then stumbled back to his seat; sweat raced from his brow. For a minute he forgot he was in the house and not an actual club.

The smoke machine malfunctioned and began to release twice the smoke at twice the rate. Puck unplugged the machine and opened the window.

"Oh shit!" he yelled, then began coughing from the smoke.

A neighbor sitting on the porch across the street panicked and called 911.

"Nine-one-one, what is your emergency?" the dispatcher asked.

"My neighbor's house is on fire and someone is home," the helpful neighbor said.

"What is the address, sir?" the dispatcher asked.

"Oh shit! I can see the flames flickering through the window."

"Sir, what is the address?" the dispatcher asked again.

Umm, sixteen-two-ten Rapahoe Street.

"Help is on the way," she assured him.

Puck returned to his seat. Maw-Maw sat on his lap and began to grind, then she stopped.

Puck pulled a fifty from his pocket and tucked it beneath one of Maw-Maw's breasts. She continued the lap dance for a moment, before returning to the mini stage. Maw-Maw grabbed the pole and pulled herself toward the top with efforts of sliding down slowly as she spiraled toward the bottom.

Puck loved it. His penis was now hard and ready for action. He did what any man would do with it: tried to put it into action.

"Sit your ass back down!" Maw-Maw shouted as she descended from the pole.

*Thump!*

Puck couldn't believe his eyes as he saw her landing. But he was too drunk and couldn't respond fast enough.

"Damn, Maw, are you all right?"

Her screeching sound was oh, so, horrifying.

Maw-Maw fell and could not move; so she laid there crying. The pain was so unbearable that she urinated on herself.

Sirens could be heard and there was a knock at the door.

"Fire department!"

Puck ran to the door butt-ass naked yelling, "Help, help! She has fallen and she can't get up!"

"Where is the fire, sir?" the fireman asked.

"Upstairs!"—Puck yelled—"Come on!"

The fireman grabbed Puck and hurried him out onto the front lawn, while the others ran to fight the fire. But when they got to the room, all they saw was Maw-Maw laying at the base of the stripper pole in her birthday suit, crying. Their eyes toured the room and in their minds, they began putting together what had taken place.

"Fire? Ain't no fire, muthafucka!" Puck spat. "If you don't get yo damn hands off me, I'm going to fuck you up Puck fashion—Westside!" Puck threw his hands in the air and signaled the fireman to come with it. "After I kick yo ass, I am going to tend to my wife," Puck told him.

Puck didn't care that he was without garments.

The fireman inside the house came outside and briefed the fire chief. The rescue crew was sent in to help Maw-Maw.

It was later learned that she had broken her hip.

Puck stayed at the hospital all night while Maw-Maw rested. He was by her side until she opened her eyes the next morning. Puck raised himself from the chair in which he'd slept.

"Maw-Maw, I have to go to work for a minute, but I'll be back," he assured her.

"Okay, baby. Don't rush back, I'll be fine. I'm okay now."

Puck kissed her on her forehead and walked off.

After going in to let his boss know that his wife was hospitalized, and that he would need a few days off, Puck stopped in to see his old friend, Paul, at That's My Dog—Norfolk, Virginia's best hotdog spot.

"Puck-Puck's in the house," Puck sang out. And he couldn't help but flirt with the fine young thang Paul had working for him.

"Paul, Maw-Maw is in the hospital. She broke her hip last night."

"Is she all right?" Paul asked.

"Yeah, she's doing better."

"How long will she be there?" Paul asked.

"About a week or two."

"Man, Puck, I am sorry to hear that brother. Is there anything I can do?"

"Just come have a drink with an ole buddy."

"Puck, you know I don't drink anymore," Paul reminded him.

"Paul, just one," Puck pleaded.

"Okay. As long as it is a non-alcoholic beverage," Paul said.

"I will be at the spot. Just come there after you get off work," Puck told him.

They both agreed and Puck; then ordered his usual fries and a tall can of sweet tea.

At the club:

The ladies were in rare form this particular evening. The finest ones were on stage and walking the floor in search of a trick for the night. Paul walked into the club feeling a little unease, being as though he hadn't been to his and Puck's old stomping ground in a while. The eye candy was dandy. Paul ordered himself a coke.

"Sorry, but we have a two-drink minimum here, sir," the waitress told him.

"But I don't drink alcohol," he informed her.

She shrugged her shoulders as if to inform Paul that she didn't give a damn, rules were rules.

"Puck, what do you want?" Paul asked.

"Get me the Puck Master," Puck replied.

"A what?" Paul asked with a puzzled look on his face.

"A mother fucking Puck Master!" Puck said matter-a-factly.

"I will have a Puck Master?" Paul ordered.

"A Puck Master? Oh my God, is something the matter with Mr. Puck?" she asked Paul.

"Why? What is a Puck Master?" Paul asked.

# Kubuki Love

"Believe me, you don't want to know," she assured him.

She grabbed a tall glass—the tallest in the house. And she brought it to their table filled with whatever the Puck Master is, and sat it beside Puck. It seemed to be what he what he would order when he would visit there.

Puck's face was buried between Dana aka Slim Thugga's legs, blowing a soft breeze on her cat, as she wound her waist to the music. Paul thought he was eating her right where she danced. Occasionally, she would slightly allow her kitten to rub his puckered lips, making her hot. It was all part of the game.

Slim danced for Puck for about forty-five minutes. Slim had a pecan complexion with a tat on her neck that read: SLIM THUGGA THE RED BONE LOVER. She was okay for a skinny girl, but Paul liked the meaty ones. Puck began to tell Paul about his and Maw-Maw's argument and how that evening had transpired. Paul couldn't stop laughing. He thought Puck was silly and a little childish at times.

"I can't believe you put a stage and a stripper pole in your room." Paul laughed. He laughed so hard he lost all of the wind in his lungs; tears rolled from his eyes with joy.

"Holdup-holdup, you mean she broke her hip trying to slide down the pole?"—he laughed harder—"And the fireman hauled you outside butt-bald naked?" Paul couldn't take it anymore, he just laughed and laughed.

"Oh my God." He smiled. "Puck, you're stupid, man. I can't believe that. That is so crazy!"

Puck quickly drank his Puck Master.

"Baby, can you bring him the second one, please. And bring me a cola, as well."

She returned with the second drink and cola.

Puck started in on that one without hesitation. Mosaic brushed by Puck, then sat in his lap. She whispered something in his ear and it looked like she was kissing his neck. Puck spoke a few words into her ear and she stroked her hand gently along his cheek, then she walked off.

"Hey look, Puck, I have to go, man. I can't spend the night in this club."

"All right, Paul, I will get with you tomorrow."

Puck had to have drunk about six Puck Masters!

"Puck-Puck, baby—Puck-Puck, baby. Awe, shuckey-duckey, Puck-Puck-Puck . . . Awe, shuckey-duckey, Puck-Puck-Puck," he sang with his hands in the air, waving them like he just didn't care. Puck was doing a dance he called the hula-hoop.

The DJ yelled, "Puck is in the house, y'all! Puck-Puck is in the house, y'all! Grab your glass if you're not a bastard and yell, fill this mother fucker with Puck Master!"

The whole club yelled, "Puck Master!"

Four of the girls in the club surrounded Puck and seductively danced with him.

"Oohwid-oohwid! Oohwid-oohwid!" Puck shouted.

Before they knew it, Puck had disrobed and began dancing in the circle of dancers, butt-naked. It was about ten minutes before the bouncers realized that he had no clothes on. Mosaic, one of the dancers, was grinding on him. She wanted him badly. She even went down on him right there in the club. Puck was a large man, and held one of the most well respected penises this side of Norfolk.

## Kubuki Love

Usually when a girl encounters Puck, two things happen: one, they wanted it; and two, they were intimidated from its size and ended up not doing him.

The bouncer snatched Puck up and shoved him outside the club, then shut the door behind him. There he stood, butt-naked in the parking lot, drunk, and the center of attention.

*Wham!*

The club door flew open.

Mosaic looked around until she spotted Puck sitting on the curb with his underwear on singing, "I'm in love with a stripper!"

She ran over to him and helped him up and helped him with his clothes. She helped Puck into her vehicle. Puck sat defenseless on the passenger side.

"Maw-Maw is hurting!" he cried.

Mosaic reached over and rubbed his penis, then said, "Oh, I plan to make maw-maw feel better."

She buckled his seatbelt and took Puck back to her place.

The ride took about fifteen minutes. She pulled into the driveway and into the garage.

She couldn't wait. She turned the car off and closed the garage door. Puck was laid-back in the seat sleeping like a baby.

Mosaic unwrapped the package she had been waiting for and wanting, since she had seen it. She nursed it with her soft lips and warm tongue, until it was hard like wine candy. To her, he tasted just as sweet, and lasted a little bit longer than the real candy.

Then she held his candy in her hand while she playfully enjoyed licking his nut sack. She became wet as she fathomed the thought of what she was going to do to this big dick that stared at her eye to eyes.

Puck eyes began to open when he noticed he was in a strange place and saw a strange woman giving him some of the best head he had ever had. Mosaic was putting it down pro-style, once she was made aware that her giving him head had awakened him. Puck aided her by moving her head with his hand in an up-and-down motion. He moaned and gyrated; then Mosaic's head popped up quickly as she wiped her face in repugnance. She couldn't believe he had just . . .

## Just Gotta Have It

"Oohwid–oohwid!" he shouted. Before you knew it, this older man named Puck had disrobed and begun dancing. Three of the girls circled this butt-naked man, and one of the dancers named Mosaic, was grinding and shaking her ass on him. She wanted him badly.

*Damn, this man has a big dick,* she thought.

She was dropping it like it was hot, when Puck grabbed her by her waist as he gyrated his hips. Mosaic just shook her ass on him. When Puck let her loose, she felt she couldn't contain herself any longer; she went down on him and gave him a quick, thirty-second blowjob.

"Hey, what the fuck?" the voice of a man said. "We can't have this shit happening. This ain't VIP, Mutha-fucka!" The bouncer immediately snatched up Puck's clothing and escorted him out of the club into the parking lot, butt-ass naked.

Mosaic was definitely intimidated by his girth; nevertheless, she just had to have it. Men with a penis size like Puck's or larger were few and far apart, and she knew that.

*Wham!*

The club door flew open. There he sat butt-naked in the parking lot, drunk, struggling to put on his clothes. Mosaic spotted Puck sitting on the curb in his underwear singing "I'm in love with a stripper!"

She hurried over to him, helped him up and helped him with his clothes. She helped Puck into her vehicle. Puck sat defenseless on the passenger side.

"Maw-Maw is hurting!" he cried.

Rory Leon

Mosaic rubbed his penis and said, "Oh, I plan to make maw-maw feel better."

She buckled his seatbelt and took Puck back to her place.

The ride took about fifteen minutes. She pulled into the driveway and into the garage. She couldn't wait. She turned the car off and closed the garage door. Puck lay back in the seat, sleeping like a baby.

Mosaic unwrapped the package she had been waiting for and wanting since she had seen it. She nursed it with her soft lips and warm tongue, until it was hard like wine candy.

To Mosaic, he tasted just as sweet if not sweeter, and longer lasting! Holding the candy she'd anticipated in her hand, she enjoyed licking his nut sack. She became wet thinking about what she was going to do to his big dick that stared her eye to eyes.

Puck began opening his eyes when he noticed he was in a strange place with a strange woman giving him some of the best head he had ever had. Mosaic's putting it down pro-style had awakened him. She was made aware that he had awakened when he placed his hand on her head, and began enjoying her skills.

He moaned and gyrated; then Mosaic's head popped up quickly and she wiped her face in repugnance. She couldn't believe he had just pissed in her mouth! Mosaic quickly aimed his hard dick toward his pants and underwear, to catch the urine.

He let out a sigh of relief after passing gas.

Mosaic, now disgusted, gazed at him with a *no-you-didn't!* glare.

"Who in the fuck are you?" Puck asked.

"Mosaic," she replied.

"Doesn't that mean mixture or something?"

90

## Kubuki Love

"Yes."

"So what are you mixed with?" Puck asked.

"My father was Black and Dominican, and my mother was Black and Philippine," she explained.

"So your father is a Bro-minican." Puck laughed.

"Take those pants off so I can wash them, and let me show you to the shower," she coached.

"I'm sorry for the accident. I didn't mean it," Puck said with a slurred speech.

"You did that shit on purpose!" she spat back, playfully.

"I feel bad," he said.

"Then come upstairs and try to make it up to me," Mosaic said softly, and led Puck's half-dressed, drunken behind to the upstairs restroom, where he was to shower. The shower was so refreshing that he stayed in there for a few extra minutes.

Mosaic slid into the shower with Puck and washed his body again for him. Softly, she rubbed his man area. *Damn, his dick is heavy!* was her notion.

"I am not digging in your ass, so I hope you cleaned it well." She looked at him in the most peculiar way.

When she was finished, they stepped out of the shower and she dried his body with a multicolored towel that read: JUST THE WAY I LIKE IT, made by designer Jau'wel.

*Mosaic's ass is phat!* Puck thought as she finished drying him off. She changed her hairstyles weekly, and this week, her hair was cut short in a bob style; which highlighted the choker she wore.

She pushed the button on the CD changer and played some soft jazz remix of old songs. Lying on her back, she pulled Puck closer as she secretly coached him to suck her breasts and kiss her stomach, gently.

Her pussy was shaven and wet; she awaited Puck's entry into private womb. She lifted his weighty penis and circled it around her wetness. Working it in slowly, she held her breath, trying to get it in completely. At first it was uncomfortable for her.

"BIG PUCK, BAY-BAY, BAY-BAY!" he yelled as he worked it.

Big Puck could use his tool well. He knew he could not force fuck the average pussy because he could possibly rip something. The sweat dripped from his chest with every gentle stroke, and with her tongue, she lapped up a bit. She moaned from the pressure of him going deeper and deeper into her with each grind.

"Is the pussy tight, baby?" she asked.

"All pussy is tight to me, baby," he said with confidence.

That shit was a turn-on for Mosaic. Her moans came more frequently until she let out an unusual giggling, screeching laugh. Puck looked at her with the look of a curious dog. You know: his ears pointed, head leaned sideways, and eyes that asked, "What the fuck was that?"

Again, she giggled.

Puck could feel the pussy getting slipperier than before. *Oh yeah, baby, Puck is in the house,* he thought

He stroked rapidly three times, then twice slow. He gyrated at a medium pace and then he hit it hard two times—*pap-pap!*

"Yeah, man," he said before he pulled it out to circle her pussy.

*Wham-pap!* He shoved it in quickly and hit it four quick pumps and two slow. Then he'd gyrate a few times, followed by the Puck's plunge! That is what he calls one of his patented maneuvers.

Her body shivered and she began to giggle. This time, she could not control this bizarre laugh. "Oooh, baby"—giggle-giggle—"that feels great!" she said, nearly out of breath.

Puck wasn't done. He had heard of this thing called the "smack, snatch, and pull" so he thought he would try it on this trick. Puck really went to work inside her walls. His penis danced wildly. He spun her onto her side and reentered her, side-mount style, with one of her legs between his and the other gripping his waist. Placing his hands on the thigh of the one leg, which was wrapped around his waist, he lifted it up and into himself, enough to play with the clitoris.

*Smack!*

He smacked her on the ass rather hard, snatched his dick out, pulled her as close as he could, while he shoveled his dick back into her pussy as far as it would go.

She almost passed out! She started giggling and shit, then she shook like a fish out of water!

*Brrrrp!* She passed gas, then cum ran down her ass cheek like the rivers flow in Mississippi. Her face buried in the pillow she tightly clutched. She wept like a young child for a good two minutes. Puck gave her a moment to cry. He was still hard! He cuddled with her for a few, rubbing her back, giving her comfort.

Gently, she kissed his chest as she pulled herself in tighter beneath his touch, like a daughter does her father. Puck knew he wasn't getting anymore pussy that night. *Damn, I should have tried to get me one,* he thought, but the liquor wasn't allowing him to ejaculate.

She rubbed his back and down along his butt, sweeping around to find that he was still hard like year-old epoxy. She knew good sex is only considered good if both parties cum.

Mosaic went downtown, destined to make him get the nut of a lifetime. She worked her tongue like the pro she was. She once was a three-time dick sucking champion at the club's all exclusive LTG (Legitimizing the Game) annual party.

She performed oral pleasures on Puck like never before. He just laid there speechless, while she enjoyed the biggest dick she had ever seen. She could barely she get the majority of his dick into her mouth, which seemed not to matter much, when concentrating on the sensitive area near the tip. Mosaic had muscles working within her mouth that most other women never knew they had.

The feeling became just what Puck wanted. He grew more and more excited with every nibble of his nuts. Tongue, lips, pulling, dancing, in, out, up and down, she put Puck in dick suckers paradise! She even sucked his dick with no hands—just straight neck!

Slurping sounds filled the room. Puck squeezed his ass cheeks tightly as a sensation ran throughout his body. He relaxed his muscles, trying to take his mind off of getting one, but that shit didn't work. He came like a horse!

Mosaic choked down the semen, nearly losing her pro status with a mild gag. Although it was a little salty and slimy, she said to him, "You taste so sweet, daddy." She peered up in his direction to see joy upon his face from his release.

Puck slept like a baby the rest of the night, and half the day away. He didn't wake until 3 PM the next day when the aroma of brunch had awakened him.

## Kubuki Love

"I got your bath water ready for you," she said. "Afterwards, your plate will be waiting for you at the table. I washed all of your clothes; they're ironed and waiting in the bathroom for you, daddy."

Puck did as instructed. He didn't remember much of the events that took place, but he could not forget Mosaic's head game. Later that day he went to visit his old friend at That's My Dog.

"Puck-Puck's in the house! Hey, Puck, where you been? And what happened to you last night?" Paul asked.

"Man! I met this badass bitch with a mean head game! She can suck a softball through a coffee straw three blocks long!"

"Dayuuum!" Paul exclaimed. "Was it like that?" he asked.

"Yes, sir. And I *must* go back!" he said, and continued. "Puck's gotsta get wit' her one-mo'-gen! She cooked, cleaned my clothes, bathed me, and it felt so damn Gooood!" Puck said with a smile.

"Puck, you stupid!" was Paul's laughter-filled reply.


Later on at the club:

"Mosaic girl, what happen to you last night?" Sunny asked.

"Girl, you remember that old dude that was at the club dancing naked?" Mosaic said.

"Yeah, the one Bubba and them threw out into the parking lot," she said.

"I brought him back to Dante's place and we got it on . . . Girl, he 'bout broke my stuff."

"What, was he knocking things over trying to walk?" Sunny asked.

"No. He was knocking the bottom out of this pussy," Mosaic assured her.

"What else?" she asked.

"Sunny girl, his dick was so heavy, and he knew just how to work it. I thought he was going to tear the lining out of my cat."

"Damn, Mo, he was that good?" she asked.

"Yeah, girl," Mosaic answered.

"You betta not let Dante find out you fucking at his house," Sunny warned.

"I am done! That dick is over. I believe I have found myself a new piece," she said, referring to Dante as being history. And she was very convincing to herself.

"Hey, Mo, I gotta see this one, and maybe we can do him together?"

"What? You wanna do a threesome, Sunny?"

"Yeah. Why not, Mo?"

"Because I am not, that's why not?" she said.

"Mo, I am not asking you to fuck me. I wanna get with him. You said he is all that."

"You know men. When two girls are in the room, it's not considered a train; it's considered a girl-on-girl-guy-watch session. I don't think so!" Mosaic explained.

"Think about it, Mo. I never had a guy with a big dick before," Sunny confessed.

"I am not sure you are quite ready for it, either, Sunny. Maybe when I am done with him, we can have him together for that one last time."

## Lil Mama

"Hey there, Lil Mama," I spoke to this fine little something with water dripping from her short frame; the wind causing a slight reaction of her nipples. She just ignored me and kept-a-steppin'. "I hate coming down to this fucking beach with all these stuck-up ass hoes."

Damn, did I say that out loud? 'Cause Lil Mama turned around and stormed in my direction.

"What did you call me, a ho?" she asked.

"Lil Mama, I just want a little conversation wit'cha, but when I spoke to you, you just kept-a-steppin'. I didn't mean no disrespect, if you didn't mean no disrespect," I said to her in a smooth, mack-daddy tone.

"What do you mean, if I didn't mean no disrespect, you didn't mean none?" she asked in a snotty tone.

"Lil Mama, it is very disrespectful when a person speaks to someone and that person doesn't return the same common courtesy. You could have at least thrown your hand up and waved or something."

"You could have come with a better line that Lil Mama one. Maybe I would have responded!" she snapped.

"A better come-on line like what?" I asked.

"Like: hello, how are you?" she responded.

I burst out laughing because that shit was funny as hell. "You call that a come-on line?" I asked her.

"Yes, I do. Treat me like a lady and not some little skank you want to go to bed with, before you get to know me."

"Okay, how about we start over then. Hello, I am Jamal. How are you doing today?"

"Fine. I am Tamika, Tamika Meyers."

"Lil Mama, . . . I mean, Tamika, are you currently seeing anyone?" I said in my gentle voice.

Tamika said, "No." Then she said, "I hate to end it here, but I really have to go. And it has been a pleasure, after all."

"Can I see you again or talk to you?" Jamal asked.

"If the time is right, then it is right," she said; then she walked off.

I was thinking what kind of storybook shit is that? As she walked away, I was hypnotized by her curves. I was taken by the swaying of her hips as she disappeared from my sight.

I thought I would never see Lil Mama again until the day I was at the bread store getting some day-old snack cakes, when she came through the door.

"Hey, Lil Mama. How are you today?" I asked.

"Fine," she said, and went about her shopping like I wasn't standing there.

"Wait a minute now, Lil Mama, I was showing you some interest over here and you just keep-a-steppin'."

"I apologize, but I am not interested," she sweetly scorned me.

"But, Lil Mama, take a second look and reconsider your actions. Maybe there is a fire burning for a relationship here."

"Hmm, maybe there could be a chance . . . let me see." She walked around me in a circle looking at my frame. "Not bad," she commented. "Not bad. Maybe I might reconsider."

"I think you should. If I was a female, I would love to date me," I said with confidence.

She smiled, but it was a smile that was like it was the first time I threw game to her. I thought the dating me line was overkill, but whatever works.

## Kubuki Love

"Why me?" she asked, then said, "And if your answer is up to par, then I will reconsider."

Then she patiently waited for my answer. I didn't know what to say. She had me on the spot. She stood there waiting to hear something crazy come out of my mouth. I went into thought for a second, but I choked. I had nothing to say so I just smiled.

"I thought so," she said.

Then she continued on with her shopping. I was stunned. I couldn't come up with anything. My mind went blank. I gave up the fight. I greeted the lady at the checkout counter before setting the items onto the counter. Lil Mama came up next to me and began setting her items on the counter as well. They were kind of close to my items. I thought she wanted me to pay for them or something.

"Thank you, sir. Have a nice day," the checkout attendant said, and handed me my change and receipt.

"How about you write your number on that receipt, and if I have reconsidered, then I will call," Lil Mama said.

Without hesitation, I wrote the number on the receipt. I noticed that Lil Mama had a nice set of breasts going on under the T-shirt she was wearing.

Several days had passed before she called. I was speechless. I got up enough nerve to ask her, "Why are you playing games?"

"Games? I am not playing games with you, Jamal. Why do you ask that?"

"Because it seems like you're not interested; then later it seems like you are."

"Well, maybe I had to feel you out before I gave in. I mean, you're nice looking, but I wasn't feeling your conversation at first."

"Oh, so you wasn't feeling my conversation at first, huh?"

"I am beginning to come around," she sweetly said.

I could hear her smiling on the other side of the phone. I returned her smile. I felt my mack beginning to take effect. We talked for half the night about nothing. On and on she talked about food.

"What if I put whipped cream all over your body and licked it off?" Lil Mama asked.

"Where did that come from?" I asked.

"Well, I just wanted to make this conversation a little more interesting. So, are you going to answer the question?"

I gathered the nerve to say, "I would be grateful; especially since no one has ever caked me up."

"Caked you up? What does that mean?" she asked, sounding all confused.

"You know, when I become your personal pancake and you glaze me up with syrups and whipped cream. I may squirm like a little bitch."

"Are you gonna try to turn me out?"

"Naw, you ain't ready for that."

"Come and find out," she challenged me. Silence fell upon the line.

"Stop playing, Lil Mama."

She said she wasn't playing; then she gave me the address to her place.

Lil Mama was waiting for me in a red, night outfit, her nipples erect and protruding from her near topless clothing. I wanted badly to touch them, pull one from its gentle wrapped position and place it within the walls of my warm mouth.

"Hi," she greeted me.

## Kubuki Love

I gave her a rose I'd bought at the gas station on my way to her place. I know it was corny and somewhat cheesy; however, I wanted to be a gentleman.

She smiled a funny looking smile, which expressed, *A rose.* And the look about her face said to me, *Nerdy, but cute.*

I wasn't sure how to take the look she was giving me. I hoped it wasn't leading toward rejection. First impressions are everything and I would have hated driving all that way to be turned around for buying a cheesy rose from a gas station.

She accepted the rose and gave me a polite, "Thank you."

I smiled, hoping that I did more help than harm.

She led me by the hand toward a room located at the rear of this well-maintained structure. It was dark as hell, and I was glad that she led the way. I felt secure.

I heard music playing and the smell of pears overtook my sense of smell. Lil Mama opened a door leading to a candle-lit tub with scented candles. Still waters filled the tub that released soft steam from its belly. Revealed, was the source of the music I heard as I was being led toward what could be considered a new experience for me.

"Take your clothes off. I want to see you," she said, as she looked into my eyes, lightly touching my chest. So I did what I think any man would do, I began to yank articles of clothing from my once-chiseled frame.

"Wait . . . wait . . . slow down. I want to watch, so do it with a little more sensuousness."

Her eyes began to shine and she put her lower lip beneath her upper teeth, biting gently. I love that particular look on women, and it rapidly caused a chain reaction in the inner soul of my britches.

Longer and wider my dick grew, until it was fully erect, slightly resembling a pirate's hook. Lil Mama giggled a cute little giggle of satisfaction. Then, with a firmness in her voice, she said, "Get the fuck in the tub."

Just before stepping in the water as ordered, she flipped a switch and bubbles began to form in the tub. Bath beads surrounded the round of my ass. The surface was slippery, like it had been lined with baby oil.

"Are you joining me?" I asked.

"No. Do you mind if I wash your hair?" she asked.

"No, I don't mind," I replied.

With slightly closed eyes, I watched this young tender thing wash every inch of my body, giving special attention where greatly needed. The suds, coupled with the warmth of the water, allowed for her bare hands to glide with ease, across the shaft of my penis. With one hand, she cupped my ball sack. Softly, she moved about her fingers, stroking my penis up and down, feeling the girth. Her taking all that was offered into the palm of her hand rendered me powerless.

This goddess controlled everything that was to happen that evening. I fell at the mercy of a perfect stranger. She could have been one of those females that got you all worked up, then slipped something in your drink and stole your kidneys. Nonetheless, kidney or no kidney, I wanted her, and the urge to have her grew stronger as the day progressed.

The warmth of the water was no contest to the warmth of her mouth. Lil Mama pulled the skin of my pecker back to a tightened position. She slowly ran her tongue across it. Easing the skin back to its rightful place, she took the tip. Ooooh! I felt fever. Her stokes became seriously soothing; her moans spoke of her wanting more. Article by article she undressed, then she pulled my dripping frame and hard pecker from the tub. I wanted to tear every article of clothing from her, but I learned that patience was king! And patience was all I had that evening.

"Get the FUCK out of the tub, Captain Crook," she forcefully said. I stepped out smartly.

*Smack!* She hit my left ass cheek.

It wasn't the type of usual smack; it was the type where her hand was like a suction cup. Smack-n-grab is what I call it.

"Turn that sweet ass around!" she ordered.

She smacked my ass again; then she spat into her hand and rubbed her clitoris. Lil Mama went straight for the doggy-style technique. She wouldn't let me just put it in and straight fuck the dog shit out of her; she was on some foreplay shit.

Lil Mama rubbed her vagina with the tip of my penis. Around and around she moved it. The pussy began to moisten until soon, it was sloppy wet. Her juices were dripping from being so wet. She began easing the head of my manhood in, a little bit at a time, until she had all of me within her.

"Yeah! Now that is what I am talking about." I was working that ass, but she wasn't moving her body.

"WHAT KINDA SHIT IS THIS?" I yelled like I was the man in charge now. "Move that ass, Lil Mama," I demanded.

Her body movement was little to none. She was just taking it in and holding on.

"I said move that ASS, Lil Mama!"

*Smack!*

I hit her on the butt. She moaned like a hurt puppy. I smacked it again and she just moaned, "Yeah, daddy."

I felt powerful; I was the man. However, she still didn't move that ass like I wanted her to. My strokes became more passionate, more dominate, more satisfying. I grabbed the scented candle and dripped droplets of hot candle wax on her ass. She moved her ass then. She began to buck like a mechanical bull.

"Oh yeah, daddy," she moaned. "I like that!"

She began to cry. She whimpered like a mutt. Lil Mama had an orgasm—not once—not twice, but three times. The last time, she grabbed my balls and squeezed them as she climaxed. I thought I was going to faint. She released her grip and I nearly fell.

Lil Mama's fingers randomly massaged my balls. Sweat beads formed on my head. My pace quickened and became sporadic. I felt the sperm making its way to the tip of my shaft. I pulled my shaft out with a quickness; it was the fastest I had seen Lil Mama move the whole night. Lil Mama turned to receive the sweetness of my coconuts. Slowly, she drank, slurping and rubbing my juices into her skin.

"Baby, you taste good." She smiled, with tears runing down her cheeks.

I had finally made it back to my apartment. I collapsed on the couch, my body quivering from weakness. The cable TV was out because some jerk off was working on the lines in our area. I hadn't had but a moment to place my keys on the counter, before the phone rang. Guess who it was: Lil Mama.

"Hey there, Lil Mama," I sang. "You miss me already?" I asked.

She sounded confused when she said, "Excuse me?"

## *Kubuki Love*

So I just played it off by saying something different. "Wassup witcha, Lil Mama?"

"Nothing. I just thought I'd call and talk to you for a minute."

"Wouldn't it be better for both of us if we talked in person?" I asked.

She chuckled; then agreed to come over to the house for a glass of ghetto wine: Wild Irish Rose.

Lil Mama came over with a tight-ass sundress on. Her hair was in a different style. In my mind, I asked myself, *Is she wearing drawers?*

Her ass jiggled slightly within her dress. The meat of her ass had me licking my chops like the wolf had done to Little Red Riding Hood. She smelled of sweet perfume; her beauty was seductive. She had done something different and I couldn't quite put my finger on it. Oh well, I'll figure it out later.

We laughed, talked, and drank until we were very intoxicated. Lil Mama was hilarious. She had tears flowing from the wells of my eyes; however, the funny thing is we never once talked about what happened earlier. It seemed to be more a bonding period and it didn't even matter to me that we'd just had sex a few hours ago.

Lil Mama fell asleep in my arms. I eased myself away from her to get a blanket to lie across her. There we lay, snuggled underneath the blanket on the sofa like lovers. I kissed her softly on her collarbone. Feeling her body against mine, stirred the desire to make nookie cookies again with her. I know she felt my penis getting hard against her.

I gyrated slightly. She began to rub me wherever her small petite fingers could go. Lil Mama pressed firmly against me with her butt imbedded in the cover of my lions. Her breasts perked like they were pointing at something across the room. I looked to see what it was they were trying to show me, but ended up just rubbing them.

Lil Mama spoke softly in my direction, "Do you have a rubber?"

I quickly replied, "Yeah!"

She placed my hand in places that told me I was in for another screwing. But something was different about her touch, it was much more sensuous. Touching her ass was like touching it for the very first time. It was cold at first, but quickly warmed up.

With her free hand she took my dick out of my pants, and began rubbing it against the walls of her vagina. That shit felt so good I started stroking it, when she whispered, "Unh-uh, let me do it." So I lay still while she played.

"Ouch! Lil Mama." Her thongs were giving my penis abrasions.

"Am I hurting you?"

"Hell, yeah! The material of your drawlers are hurting me!"

She removed them and continued. "Is that better?" she asked.

"Yeah, that's much better"

Lil Mama began to insert the tip of my penis into her throbbing, wet pussy. Anticipation was killing me. I wanted to be in control of the stroke. I wanted all of me inside of her. She took her time and gave it to me slowly.

*Smack!*

I whacked that ass one good time.

*Smack!*

I whacked that ass again.

"Stop!" she yelled.

"What?" I questioned.

"I don't like being slapped on the ass!"

"Huh?"

*You were loving it a minute ago,* I thought. This sure is some freaky shit! But I am with it. I didn't slap that ass anymore, but I was laying down the pipe. I busted all over Lil Mama's ass. She rubbed it into her flesh with two fingers; then she stuck those fingers in her mouth.

"You taste good."

Dude, I fell right to sleep! I woke up the morning after and Lil Mama was gone. What was I to do? I took me a long shower and made myself a bite to eat.

Feeling a little closer to Lil Mama, I decided to take her some flowers. When I got there, she was kneeling in the flowerbed, picking at something.

"Here, Lil Mama."

"Awe, that is so sweet of you," she cried. She hugged me tightly. Her hand moved along the crease of my back in a sexy way.

"Come in for a minute while I clean up a bit."

She opened the door for me. While I was waiting for her, I walked toward the fireplace and perused the pictures on the mantle. Lil Mama came into the room.

"Looking at my pictures, huh?"

"Yeah," I confessed.

So she began to explain: "This is my daughter and her friends. This one is me at a Christmas party."

"What? Daughter?" I said in shock.

"Yeah, my daughter Tammy!" she yelled from the bottom of the stairs. "Tam, come down here for a minute. I want you to meet someone."

*DAYUUUM!!*

To my surprise they looked like twins. Almost the same in every aspect. My mouth dropped to the floor. Both of them were just as surprised to see me as I was them. I fucked both of them in the same day. I couldn't choose between the two of them, so I chose neither. The mama I felt was best, but I didn't go there again, although, she did fuck me better. And I was loving that freaky-dominatrix shit. But on the other hand, I was also loving the way Tammy was sexing me: slowly; and being patient with the pussy was the first for me. Okay, okay, okay, I can't lie. The devil made me do it again, and again, and again. Damn, Lil Mama, why yah do me like yah do, do, do?

## Literally

Sometimes I think stereotypic statements are true. For example: men think about sex every fifteen seconds. This is impossible, and I understand it is based on an average and not an actual. Fifteen seconds is far-fetched, but fifteen minutes is more realistic. Then there are many that are not true like: all black people eat chicken and watermelon. This is close to being true, but I met a few that changed my mind.

I think about sex everyday, but not every fifteen seconds. I believe in my mind that I want to have sex everyday, whether it is oral or physical; however, if I were to have sex everyday, it would change the way I thought about it.

This day, I was thinking about sex hard. My penis hardened as I walked to the kitchen to get a cold beer. There was something going on within me that wouldn't let me think of anything else. The phone rang.

"Hello?"

"Hi, what are you doing?" April asked.

"I was thinking about you," I said.

I knew it wasn't what I was really thinking, but it wasn't all a lie. I should have been truthful and said I was thinking about fucking someone; then you called. I wonder what she would have said after hearing the truth.

Then she asked, "What about me were you thinking?"

Then it came out, "I was thinking about coming over and fucking you until our bodies weaken and your muscles shake uncontrollably."

Then April said something that changed my whole mood. "What time will you be here?"

"Six fifteen," I replied.

I jumped in the shower to clean myself thoroughly, making sure I hit all the hot spots twice. I splashed on my favorite cologne and drank another beer before dashing to my car. I had to stop by the store to get a few things, including some chewing gum, so the beer wouldn't be the first thing she smelled. I wasn't sure what type of prophylactic to use, Magnum was too big and a regular size was really too small.

"Awe, fuck it, I will go for the small boys. Ain't no use in fronting."

April was wearing shorts and a wifebeater when she opened the door. She kissed me and told me to come in. The television was loud as hell and she was watching Lifetime. She turned the TV off and turned the radio on.

"Can I get you anything?" she asked.

"No, thank you," I leaned back on her bed.

"When I asked if I could get you anything, I wasn't speaking of a beverage, I was talking about me."

"Well, in that case, I will take one large order of get the fuck over here. I will have a five-minute sucking to go with that a handful of ass. Super-size that ass for me. I have an appetite tonight."

She chuckled, "What do we have here?"

She reached into my pants and began to play with my penis. I did, at this time, what any man would have done in my shoes—I put my hands behind my head and began to relax, while she worked it. I grew about four inches longer and ten times harder within seconds.

## Kubuki Love

She wasted no time getting it up. She pulled off my clothes. I stood beside her with all my nakedness extended into her hand. April knew what I liked; she massaged my nuts, then moistened the tip of my penis with her tongue. My balls became relaxed before they were all drawn up and tight.

"Yeah, I like it when the balls are relaxed," I told her. "It makes the cum flow easier."

She said nothing; she just continued with the hand job. It was feeling so good I had to look away and focus on something in the room, just to take my mind off things.

*Awe, sheiit!*

A push of warmth overcame my penis. My dick stiffened to protect itself from the wet beating it was taking from her mouth. Again, I did what any man in that case would have done. I grabbed the back of her head.

It became harder and harder to focus. I had even turned the radio up. I began thinking about what I had to do the next day, but none of that worked. I knew if I didn't stop her, my evening would end short. Let's face it, she gives good head. I pulled her head away.

"Am I hurting you?" she asked.

"Yes, but in a good way," I replied. "You were about to make me get one."

I reached down between her legs and caressed her monkey. She was sloppy wet, her juices dripped from my fingers. It was grossing me out, so I pulled my hand away and dried it instantly. I did the same thing with the head of my penis. The outside of her vagina was wet and warm. Easing in it was not a difficult task.

"Damn, girl, you're wet as hell!"

With my penis in hand, I rubbed the outside in full circles; then I pushed it inside her a little. I circled the walls, then worked it again. I did this until I was about to take full strokes within her. This was driving her crazy. Her body moved as I circled her clitoris. She was anticipating me inserting it within her. But I would switch it up on her and circle the opposite way. I could feel that she wanted it more and more, until it made her climax.

Cheating her, I hadn't gotten one yet, so she had to pay up. I made April lay on her side with one knee lying near her chest. I put Mr. Chocolate back in as smoothly as I could. I began with small, easy strokes, and then moved on to long easy strokes. Her waist was there as a stabilizer for the punishment. Her moans quickly ascended to cries of passion. Stroking her asshole gently only sweetened the pot. I did what any man would have done—I switched positions.

"Lay on your stomach," I commanded.

I mounted her with my chest on her back. I called this one the six o'clock style. That's when we both lay in a straight position and I'm inserted from the back.

"Ooooh, yeah, momma, right there."

That pussy was feeling too good. Sweat dripped from my face to her back. She began breathing heavily; her muscles tightened and her moans became screams.

"Stop. Stop." She pushed me off.

"What's the matter, baby?" I asked.

"You are beating my pussy up; it got dry."

So I did what any man would have done in this situation—I looked down at my throbbing member.

"You got to do something, because I haven't cum yet."

"You haven't?" she asked.

Without hesitation, she went to work. I think her mouth feels better than her pussy. She had to have sucked my dick for at least fifteen minutes. I felt like something was wrong, because I wouldn't have lasted five minutes with her sucking my dick on a normal day.

April stopped. She complained about her mouth and jaw hurting. "Are you trying to give me lockjaw?" she asked.

"No, I just came to do what I said I was going to do." My response was confident. "I guess that means there's only one other thing left to do."

"What?" she asked, wearing a confused look.

"Bend that ass over," I said.

I reached for the jar of petroleum she kept on the dresser. I lubricated my shaft with it and told her to relax her muscles. She was in disbelief, but she went along with it. I greased her anal area as well. Do the words "fits like a glove" mean anything to you?

It was like something I had never witnessed before. She moaned but didn't move. The tightness and the warmth would soon bring me to my knees. I felt like I was going to buckle like Roy Jones in a light heavy weight fight.

Her ass was as smooth as silk. I played around with it for a second. It was time to see what was really good. I turned the lights on so I could see.

April was in the doggy-style position when I said to her, "Part those cheeks, ma."

Her asshole widened to the exact size of my dick. I stuck my dick in, and watched it go in and out and out and in. The feeling was like no other. I grabbed the shaft of my chocolate stick. I twisted my crookedness until it was facing downward. I lunged inward, putting all of me inside of her. I moaned, twisted it and lunged forward.

I had to let go of it and hold her waist to finish out my strokes. I was nearing the climax of this century. It began to slide in and out better than before; it felt as slippery as her pussy.

"Awe . . . yeah, ma, I like that."

She held the pillow tightly in her hands . . . her teeth gritted, her hair was a mess, her ass cheeks rippled with every stroke. It was feeling so good, but then I looked down because I smelled something awful. It was covered in shit! I mean, literally, covered—from the head of my dick to the root of my pubic hair—nothing but waste. I pulled out and rushed into the bathroom to wipe myself clean. I put my on pants and left, all the while, April was on my heels.

"Did I do something wrong?"

"No."

"Then why are you leaving?" she asked.

"Because . . . I just have to go."

"Did I satisfy you?"

I was out the door.

It turned my stomach a few times to smell the foul odor which embedded my genital area. I didn't even get me one before the odor brought me to my knees. I didn't call her for several days after. I guess you can say that, I fucked the shit out of her—literally.

## Who the Phuck Is That?

I was sleeping like a baby when I was awakened by a rapid knock at the door. It was 3:17 AM. I remember my first reaction was to look at the clock, so I could say the time when I cursed out the idiot banging on my door at that time of the morning.

The first thing out of the bed was my feet, of course, as I swung them around in unison to the floor. I noticed blue and red lights flashing outside of my window. I felt as if I was moving in slow motion. My body became heavy. It seemed as if I could barely reach the door.

I grabbed the handle to the door and pulled it open as fast as I could. All of a sudden, there was a flash of a bright white light. I was staring into a flashlight. I grabbed for my chest, but it felt like it wasn't there. My knees buckled, rendering me helpless. I was kneeling in a helpless position; my head bowed as if I were hit with an iron rod.

"Stand up, son!" said the thunderous voice I heard.

Feeling I couldn't stand to my feet didn't keep me from trying. Although feeling physically weak, I stood to my feet. The movement was similar to that of a newborn horse: kind of wobbly at first, then stabilized.

Once I made it to my feet, an embrace filled with love overwhelmed me. No one was present, but I could feel something hugging me. A strong sensation, an overabundance of love poured out, covering me from head to toe. It's hard to explain the feeling at this particular time; nonetheless, it felt like the love of God was blessing me. The feeling was so strong, my body collapsed. I was left hunched over and crying.

*Crackle-pop-crunch!*
*Crinkle-bing-snap!*
*Doon-ping-errrk!*
"Stand up, son!"

This time I couldn't! I felt pain! The pain came from my chest when I heard the commotion outside my window. I remember now, as it became clearer to me. It was all coming back to me as I recalled the events.

The knocking at the door was the bass blasting loudly as I turned the volume up on my stereo. I saw a police car quickly approaching, which must have been the blue and red lights I saw flashing.

I looked at the clock on my radio as I reached to turn it down and throw the liquor bottle under the passenger's seat. I swung my feet around in unison. I rose up, using the steering wheel for leverage, and it turned. That must have been the doorknob I thought I yanked.

It seemed as if it took so long to get to the upright position, due to the heaviness of my drunken body. The bright lights . . . Oh, those bright lights were so brilliant, they blinded me. The lights were from the headlights of the car I'd just hit; badly injuring the family of five inside the oncoming car!

I cried uncontrollably and pleaded my sins to God. Jesus saved me right there on the spot, cleansing my soul and spirit, making me a new man!

"Jesus! Yes—yes, Lord!" I cried out, feeling the anointing of his blessings overtaxing my soul.

The rumbling of metal was the crackle-pop-crunch! Crinkle-bing-snap! Doon-ping-errrk! I'd heard.

The police and rescue persons used the Jaws of Life to free the family from their vehicle. The second "Stand up son," was actually a trooper yelling at the people to stand aside as he ran down the embankment to save me. But it was too late, Jesus had already done that for him!

The pain in my chest was the steering wheel that my chest had wrapped around. I cried unto the Lord, "Lord, forgive me! I'll never do it again. I'm so sorry, Lord. Please forgive me!"

After my 18-month recovery in the rehab and 7 years in jail for involuntary manslaughter, a young man holds the door of the church open for me, for Sunday morning service. Tears filled the wells of my eyes as I thanked him for being kind. With both hands on the wheels of my chair, I journeyed into a new life—this time with God!

The family of five I now grieve for is a broken family with three remaining. Lost were the husband, the provider of his family, and one of their 10-month-old twins. The others were left mangled, both mentally and physically.

I live with this every day. I can't forgive myself for what I have done. I can't bring myself to face the remainder of their family. I cry myself into a depressive sleep, wishing that my life was the one taken. Knowing that I took the innocent lives of others, because I thought drinking and driving was cool, condemns my soul. I will never ever be the same again. Lord, forgive me!

## Chocolate Crème Deluxe
## Six Months Later . . .

Rebecca was stunning! Her hair was done; it lay slightly across her face. Her lips were glossed gently; her face glowed like a new penny in the sun. It is a beautiful thing . . . another one of God's perfect imperfections! She is a smart and sweet person.

Dinner looked wonderful. She prepared my favorite: Macaroni and cheese with shrimp and broccoli, fried pork chops, and biscuits with honey!

Umm-umm.

"I have a little something planned for us tonight," she said.

"What?" I asked.

"You will see."

"I guess."

"First, we gotta go to the mall. I need somethin' special for tonight."

"Dayuuum! It's like that?"

"Yeap. Hope you enjoy it!"

"I'm sure I will."

"Do you want a hint?"

"Yeah."

"Well, it is a fantasy of mine that guys . . . Naw, I ain't gonna say."

"Come on! Tell me."

"Naw! That's all right. You'll have to wait to see."

Rebecca had my mind guessing, my curiosity aroused! I was hungry as hell, so we had to stop by this fast-food spot that carried Coney Island. (If you don't know what they are, then you need to ask somebody!) Despite the fact that she had already cooked, I had to munch on something until we reached the house again.

The mall was packed with people of all kinds. It was like a festival. There were sample concessions everywhere! Folk licking their fingers, ladies dressed in the skimpiest outfits, guys spitting game, trying to get their mack on. It's funny being in a public place with someone that society considers less fortunate, such as Rebecca being vertically challenged and all. But as I said before, she is stunning!

Rebecca had me wait in the Wrecka-Stow looking for her a special CD she called *Marvin Sease*. She said there was a song on the CD called "Candy Licker"; it was the song she was to play for this evening.

There were girls around everywhere looking good as a muthafucka. She came back around with about five bags of shit. I thought, *Damn, girl, what the fuck is you going to do tonight?* I was anxious to get started with my little surprise. We finished walking the mall before heading back to the parking lot to retrieve our ride home.

"The food looks lovely Rebecca. You out did yourself, girl." Rebecca smiled and then asked what I thought about tonight.

I said, "I don't know."

She asked if she could do anything to me she wanted, then she took the bone of the pork chop, stuck it in her mouth, and slowly sucked it like it was me. My mind danced wildly with imagination of what was to be.

"What do you plan on doing?" I asked.

"Never you mind. I just want to know what my options were."

"Options?" I questioned.

"Yeah, options!"

"Why, what do you mean by that?"

She looked me eyeball to eyeball and said to me, "If I want to pluck your balls while I suck your dick, can I?"

I smiled and paused for a brief moment before answering that one, and then confidently I said, "Yeah."

She continued, "If I want to shove my finger up your ass while I ride that dick, may I?"

I yelled, "Hell naw! With those fat-ass stubs . . . sheiit, you won't be poking me in the ass with those mini dick-skinners!"

She laughed uncontrollably at my facial expressions.

"What if I wanted to lick the crack of your ass?" she asked.

I smiled a smile that told her I was with that, then she said, "And I will use some honey."

My dick began to get hard from the words she spat. She was getting me anxious to receive the night's promises. I felt a poop coming on; my stomach began to reject all that I had eaten that day. Rumble bubbles began to form. I held my ass cheeks tightly in the closed position, trying hard not to let loose the gasses that began to seep from my sphincter.

"May I be excused? Baby, I have to use the restroom for a minute." I hated taking a dump over someone's house, but I had to do what I had to do.

As soon as I got up from the chair, one came down—prrrrrrb!! I felt a little embarrassed that she might have heard that, but it was a bit too late, it came out, anyway. I hurried to the restroom to get on the toilet. I was moving so fast, I didn't even feel her on my heels. I rushed in, closed the door behind me, yanked my pants down around my ankles, and took a squat on the john.

The first one came out almost before I sat down; then the door opened slowly. I grabbed my private, trying desperately to cover it before she saw it.

"What are you doing in here?" She walked over to me without answering my question; she removed my hands from covering my private and began to give me a blowjob!

*Oh shit!*

I didn't know what to do. She wasn't on her knees; she stood between my legs sucking me off, while I was taking a shit. My legs extended themselves in front of me until I felt a shit coming out. I moaned like a bitch! "Unnnh, shit!"

Oh shit, a turd dropped.

*Plunkit!*

"Oh yeah," she moaned. Slurping and moaning she reached those small stubby-ass hands into toilet and grabbed my nuts and began to massage them. I looked down, all I could see was her head going up and my dick was feeling better than it has ever felt before.

I was confused. I wasn't sure if I wanted to drop another turd or cum. My mind began to play tricks on my ass. The turd would come down, and just when I thought it was going to drop, it went back up. The head was intensifying to the point of precum. I learned from this that you can't have a bodily function and cum at the same time, figure that? I squeezed that last turd down; when it made its approach toward the exit—
*Plunkit!*

She moaned again, "Oh yeah, baby. You taste so sweet."

I couldn't help myself. It was hard to keep from busting a nut once that last turd had come out. From the belly of my scrotum, it ascended to the tip of my dick . . . she drank it like it was milk. That shit was nasty, but it felt great!!

She called what she had just done a "Plunkit." Next, she eased me off of the throne into the shower. She washed me from head to toe first with a washcloth. Then she used her lips, accompanied by her tongue, and that got my dick rock hard again. She climbed on me looking like a Koala bear, trying to go up the tree. She was heavy as hell; my knees nearly buckled from holding her ass up. I carried her right to her bedroom dripping wet, and began to fuck her little ass where she lay.

I heard something that sounded like the front door opening. "Shhh! You hear that? Someone just came in the house."

"I know. I invited a friend over to join us, and that's who just came in." The door to the bedroom opened and the silhouette of another female midget appeared. I didn't even question. I knew what was about to go down in the dark, slightly moon-lit room.

I stopped my stroke and relaxed on the bed. Rebecca began to kiss the other midget. I watched for a second, stroking my penis, keeping it hard while they enjoyed themselves for a minute. One of them grabbed my dick. I couldn't tell which of them it was; I just knew the grip was tight.

A tingling sensation came over my body. Rebecca and her friend tongued each other with my dick between their mouths. It was feeling so good that I wanted to cum right there on the spot, but I wasn't going out like a punk, though. A chance like this only comes once in a nugka's lifetime. I was going for the extended rounds! I wanted this to last all night. Two midgets at once, shit yeah! It was fuel for the fire that burnt to keep this night oil lit.

One started to lick my balls as the other one gave head. They continued licking and sucking inches of my body that I never knew had sensitivity. I squirmed with passion. I was ready to bust, but "I am a champ!!" Ain't no bitches making me bust my nuts from a blow-job!

I rolled Rebecca off of me and began to return the favor. I licked her clit, and when it got wet enough, I put my chin into it. I moved my chin smartly about: a little chin and little tongue; I continued that for a good thirty seconds. She got excited and pulled my chin closer and began to work her hips. Rebecca held my ears with those stubby-ass fingers, winding her waist, making these weird-ass noises. The noises stopped quickly when that other midget kissed her in the mouth and pinched her tits.

Midget number two took off some clothes, and then softly told Rebecca to get in the doggy-style positions, so I could work it. She complied and I worked her ass like a porn star. Midget number two enjoyed a slight taste of my heresy highway. Midget two tossed my salad with something. I couldn't tell what it was, but I imagined it was that honey Rebecca spoke of earlier.

I arched my back, giving all my ass to midget two. She licked my asshole clean, then added more dressing for my salad; it eased along the crack of my ass. Rebecca wrapped her legs around my waist and with me inside her, she gyrated.

There I stood in the doggy-style position with one midget licking my ass, and the other grinding on my dick. Dayuuum, that shit was the bomb! My climax was near and I had to let them know that they had brought this giant to his knees.

"I'm about to cum," I said.

I felt midget two grab my balls and rotate them, spreading my butt cheeks with the other hand. I thought, *Hell yeah! Midget two is about to eat of the fruit I bare.*

My cum was closer and closer to escaping my shaft. "Oh . . , ohh . . . ohhh, God! Ohhhh!!" My knees buckled and my release shot a line across Rebecca. I felt hands squeezing tightly the fat of my ass.

"Ohhhh!!" I moaned. Ohhh, shit! Ohhhh, God!" I called. "God, help me!" I yelled.

And with one swift kick, I kicked the shit out of midget two. That muthafucka rolled off the bed onto the floor and grabbed her stomach, lying in the fettle position.

I remember putting my foot on the chest of that drag queen, midget bitch, trying to pull his pecker off. I beat the shit out of that midget, freak bitch!

When the cops arrived, I had nearly beaten both of them to death. Rebecca must have called them before trying to get me off of her friend. I knocked both of their asses out; I left in handcuffs on a stretcher.

The hospital had to put twenty stitches in my ass that night. That midget fucker had a pecker the size of John Holmes! I never saw it coming—go figure! I almost passed out from the penetration. It took all I had to get him off me. I am so embarrassed! That shit made the fucking front page of the news! I got fired from my job and my landlord calls me a drag queen, and issued me a 30-day eviction notice.

### Kubuki Love

My mother called and told me my family was calling her left and right, telling her they didn't know I was into drag!

When I get out and find that midget bitch, I am going to kill her and that frosted mini freak!!

## SEVEN

## Seven's Haven "911"

"Nine-one-one, what's your emergency?"

"I am bleeding!"

"Where are you bleeding, sir?"

"I am too embarrassed to say."

"Were you shot or stabbed?"

"No! But it sure feels that way."

"You are calling from a cell phone, sir. Where are you?"

"I am at one, seven Billings Street in Norfolk, sitting on the porch of an abandoned house."

"Okay, sir. Help is on the way."

"Thank you very much . . ."

The police and ambulance arrived to the scene.

"What is your name, sir?"

"Artest Calkins."

"Mr. Calkins, what happened?"

"I am too embarrassed to say. I just need to go to the hospital!"

Officer David shined his light on Artest's clothes and noticed that his pants were wet. With what, he had no idea.

"Do you have any ID?" Officer David asked.

"Yes, sir," Artest moaned, as he rose up to retrieve his wallet from his soaked pants. He handed his ID to the officer. The wallet smelled of urine and crap.

"Sir, can you open it and remove your ID?" Officer David asked. "Thank you! Sir, do you know who did this to you?"

"Yes."

"Who, sir?"

"I rather not say."

"If you don't tell us, then how can we help you?"

"Look, bro, I just want some medical attention, that is all. I am not asking to press charges. I just want to see a doctor."

"Okay, sir."

The ambulance attendant rushed to Artest's aid only to learn . . .

His doorbell rang.

"Who is it?"

"Pizza delivery!"

"I didn't order no damn pizza. Who is it?"

"Pizza delivery!"

"For who?"

"Seven!"

"Seven?" Artest opened the door to see a highly frustrated pizza delivery man, holding a pizza.

"How much?" Art asked.

"It was paid for in advance."

"Well, let me at least give you a tip."

Artest took out his wallet and gave a five spot to the pissed off pizza man.

"Thank you, sir, and have a nice day," he said.

"You as well," the pizza man said.

Artest closed the door, then he opened the box. The aroma of this piping hot pizza made him hungry. Being as though he hadn't eaten as of yet, he thought the timing was perfect.

Artest looked at the box for the name, and noticed there was a note that read: TONIGHT IS YOUR NIGHT, SEVEN. Below that, there was a number.

Artest picked up the phone and dialed the number.

"Economy. This is Ahmon, how may I help you?"

"Economy? What is this?" Artest asked.

## Kubuki Love

"A hotel, sir. Is there a guest you're trying to reach?" Ahmon asked.

"Yes. Do you have a Seven listed as your guest?"

"Wait, please," the Arabian man asked and put the call through.

"Hello," the seductive voice greeted.

"Hey, this is Art. Thanks for the pizza."

"Fuck that . . . getcho ass over here!"

"Excuse me?"

"Tidewater Drive; next to the BK. Room two eighteen. The door is open!"

*Click!*

Artest had just remembered when and where he had met Seven. He also recalled how gorgeous she is. Wearing red lipstick that popped because of its high gloss, she had on high heels with the straps that criss-crossed up her leg. Her matching dress fit firmly, which decorated her ass and added a succulent appeal to her breasts.

So he got on his bicycle and rode it up the street to the hotel. He lived on Lindenwood Street, in a duplex that sat on the corner. It was barely a mile up the road, and he was thanking the Lord that she didn't summons him to the Motel 6 on Military Highway. That would have been a hump.

Art opened the door slowly, only to see Seven brushing her hair, wearing nothing!

"Close the door, Art. Do you want all of Hampton Roads to see me?"

"No, ma'am. I want all of that for my eyes only."

Art walked over to the mirror where she stood, and placed his hands on her ass.

*Smack!*

He didn't know what hit him.

"You smell of outside! Getcho freaky ass in the shower!" she spat.

"Whatcha smack me for?"

"Because I didn't say you could touch me, yet!"

"What the fuck am I here for?"

*Smack!*

"Didn't I say getcho ass in that shower? And hurry up because I ain't about to fuck no stankin'-ass nug-ka!"

Art held his cheeks and stared at her for a second. He was thinking, *I should fuck her up. She has one more time to do that shit again.*

Seven knew that she had him when he didn't hit her back. She began to help him undress. First the jacket, then the shirt . . . *Artest is nice looking! His chest is firm. Six pack. Damn!* she thought.

The belt was next. She copped a feel as she lowered his pants, maintaining her composure when she felt the size of his dick. Holding it in her hand, she bent her legs. And with an opened mouth, she pulled it closer. Art closed his eyes so he could enjoy the pleasure she was about to give. She blew a soft, gentle air on the head on his dick. Art opened his eyes to see what had just happened. He imagined he was about to get himself a BJ. That's where his mind was.

"You must shower first, baby. Then I will blow more than your mind."

Art hurried into the shower to wash his body clean from the scent of the outdoors. Seven stood naked in the doorway of the bathroom.

"Pull the curtain open while you wash!" she demanded.

## Kubuki Love

Art opened the curtain as he was asked to, and Seven yelled out, "Put some more soap on that rag, bitch!"

"What?"

"Does your nasty ass need me to come in there and wash you?" she questioned.

"No, I can handle this on my own! Thank you."

"Humph!" she gasped. "Dig in that ass! What if I want to lick you there? Bend over and dig, bitch ass!" She added.

"Wow, Seven! Where is all of this aggressiveness coming from?"

"Shut up, bitch! I ask the questions! That is my dick tonight! My ass tonight! And if you don't like it, then get your shit and get the fuck out! And if you do get the fuck out, you will not have to worry about ever getting this ass! So either get out or get busy!"

Art didn't even have to think that one through.

"Get busy!"

*I mean, how bad could name-calling be? I am about to tear this pussy up! She will be calling me daddy in about five minutes,* Art thought.

"Now getcho ass out of that shower, bitch, and come to the bed!" Seven said as loud as she could, and turned and walked over to the bed. Seven knew she would have to work him to keep him on her team.

Art got out and grabbed a towel.

"I didn't say dry off, did I? I like it wet!" she said.

Art came in the room dripping wet.

"Lay on the bed!" she commanded.

Seven nursed his dick with her mouth without sucking, teasing it until it was rock hard. Art moaned, then requested that Seven put it her mouth. She took it in like a champ! Art was in heaven, or so he thought, until Seven stopped.

"What, baby? Why you stop?" he questioned.

Seven playfully stroked his dick before she placed a condom on it; then she mounted it. The fit was perfect. Seven reached between his legs and fondled his balls. This excited Art to cum.

"Fuck!" Seven yelled. "Bitch, did you cum?"

"Yeah . . . that was great!" Art smiled.

"Bitch, you ain't Tony the Tiger." Seven dismounted what she thought was the perfect size dick.

Art gathered his penis into his hand and headed to the bathroom in a rush. He didn't even take the rubber off, he just began to pee. The condom filled with urine and semen, and its weight caused it to automatically slide from the base of his shaft directly into the toilet. *Thunk!*

"You nasty!" Seven said as she watched him. "That was so man of you to piss in the condom."

With the rag he washed with, he cleaned his penis.

"See, all to the good!" he commented.

Art lay across the bed to take a brief rest. "I'll be ready in a minute for another round. That bike ride must have gotten me a bit fatigued."

"Oh, is that so?" she asked.

Art knew he had her attention with the size of his dick and how good it made her feel—so he thought. His confidence was high; he smiled as he drifted off into a deep sleep.

The cool, wet-simulated feeling from petroleum jelly began to awaken Art. The massaging of his balls brought forth the smile he wore, until she eased one of her fingers into his ass. His eyes shot open, he jerked his body and tightened his ass cheeks, only to learn that

Seven had handcuffed his ankles to his wrists, and tied the cuffs to the door's handle. Another rope was anchored from the cuffs to the bed.

"Hey-hey, Seven, baby, what is this?"

"Nothing!"

"What do you mean 'nothing'? I am not into all of this freaky shit!"

"What freaky shit?"

"This shit!" he yelled while shaking the cuffs.

"Oh, that freaky shit . . . Bitch, that ain't freaky, that's just how Seven gets down. You betta ask somebody."

"Ask who?" Art asked.

Seven reached between his legs and pulled his dick to the back as he lay in a helpless fetal position. With rubber gloves on, she pulled on his dick, up and down, numerous times. Art's dick got hard again. She couldn't fight the urge to put it in her mouth once more.

"Damn! This is some good-ass head," Art mumbled.

Seven eased her finger in his ass again.

"Woooo," Art said.

Art didn't know whether to fight it or invite it. He relaxed his ass muscles and got into it. She slurped and gulped his large dick. Art chuckled when she gagged from trying to take it all in. He knew that unless she was a deep-throat artist, she wasn't going to get all of it down. Most girls don't know how to relax their throat to take it all in. She tickled his balls and played in his ass with her finger.

"Damn! That feels good, baby. I am feeling a little suspect, though!"

Seven took in his words and returned with a few of her own, "And this big dick tastes so good. Ummm! Ummm!" she slurped.

Seven got up from the bed and walked over to the dresser. She opened up the drawer and removed a penis strap-on device, and a small, vibrating dildo.

"Oh, hell-to-the-no! Let me loose!"

*Smack!*

"Shut up, bitch!"

Art tightened his ass cheeks so she couldn't get it in.

"You're never gonna get it," he said, sounding like that song by those girls.

"Don't make me, Art!"

"Don't make you, what?"

"I know how to get it in!" she exclaimed.

"NO!" he cried out.

Seven placed that greasy-ass penis up to his tightened ass cheeks. She put her hands on his thighs and pulled his cheeks apart, while she pushed her pelvis.

Nothing. He was much too strong.

*Thump!*

She thumped his balls.

His asshole began to be more accessible. He squeezed this time, with his penis touching his asshole.

*Thump!*

She shoved it in. Art began to quiver as she worked it in and out, as if she were a man. Her hips gyrated as she got more into it.

*Smack!*

She hit his ass and yelled, "Whose ass is this?"

"Yours!" he moaned.

*Smack!*

"Whose, bitch?" she asked again.

"Yours, Seven—Yours!"

"Yeah, bitch! You betta recognize."

Seven worked his ass over and continued with her shit talking, "Where's the cum at now, you minute muthafucka? Big-ass dick and can't even use it! What a fucking waste of good dick! You know what? I am going to show you how to put it down when you holding a lil something-something. Huh? Yeah!"

Seven was wearing his ass out. Art couldn't even talk; he began losing consciousness.

"Hang in there now!" Seven fondled his balls.

A weakened scream was all he could muster before blacking out. Art woke up at 3:13 AM—butt-ass naked, with part of the pizza receipt taped to his dick that read: THANK YOU. COME AGAIN.

He had reached the highest point of climax without notice. He gathered his belongings and proceeded out the door. His asshole was throbbing.

"Fuck!" he yelled, followed by a faint mumble, "Somebody done stole my ride."

Art walked until he couldn't walk anymore, so he sat on a porch and dialed 9-1-1. He wasn't much more than a block away from his home.

"Nine-one-one, what's your emergency?"

"I am bleeding!"

"Where are you bleeding, sir?"

"I am too embarrassed to say."

"Were you shot or stabbed?"

"No! But it sure feels that way."

"You are calling from a cell phone, sir. Where are you?"

"I am at one, seven Billings Street in Norfolk, sitting on the porch of an abandoned house."

"Okay, sir. Help is on the way."

*Rory Leon*

"Thank you very much . . ."

## Puck

The door opened. "That's my dog!" Puck screamed, with both of his hands extended toward the sky.

"Come on in and have a seat, Puck," Crème welcomed. "How are you doing today and what will you have?"

Puck never ordered more than fries and a lemon iced tea. He was there more so for moral support of Mr. P's business and conversation with him, rather than to have a full meal. He referred to the restaurant as "the barber shop," a place where he could come and kick it with is old friend.

"Mr. P," Crème continued, "I need to leave for the day. I have to take my brother to the doctor for an appointment.

"Sure, Crème, just take care of your business and I will see you on tomorrow."

"Thank you, Mr. P." Crème held her hand over her mouth to fight back the tears, because the thought of her brother being ill, came as a sudden strike to the head. She hugged his neck tightly as she struggled to gather herself. The scent of his skin took her mind to another dimension.

Crème untied her apron and hung it on the hook in the back. Puck elbowed Paul, and with a smirk he chanted, "The Lord is my shepherd and he knows what I want!"

Playfully shoving Puck back, he said, "Stop looking at that girls butt, Puck!"

"Man, she got a nice one!" he smiled. "Bye, Ms. Crèmella Caliente," he said, as she walked out of the door.

Crème just smiled at Puck's silliness.

"Um-umph, what I would do to that one!" Puck thought.

"P, I have to get out of here and get back to work. I'll catch up with you later." On that note, Puck slapped P five and left.

His cell phone chirped, and chirping meant there was a text message waiting for him in his inbox. He retrieved the message and found it was from Seven. It read: HEY, BABY, COME SEE ME AT 9634 9TH BAY, UNIT 6. I AM WAITING! -7-

"I love when they call me Big Puck-Puck!" he sang to the tune of a Biggie song, as he headed in that direction.

She met Puck at the door fully dressed, looking like a librarian. "Hola, papi. Como esta usted?"

"Muy bien, baby, muy bien!" was Puck's reply.

"Come on in and make yourself comfortable," Seven offered.

"Why thank you, honey. Don't mind if I do. Where would you like me to sit?"

"Come into the bedroom, where I am," she coached.

"Okay." Puck walked into the room and noticed the TV was playing porn.

"My damn dick is getting hard!" Puck exclaimed. "Turn that shit off. It's making me horny."

"Did you take your Viagra, pops?"

"Pops . . . you won't call me pops when I am popping that ass. And I don't need any Viagra because my dick stays hard like . . . Oh my God! I need some bubble gum," Puck sang.

"Get your old ass naked then," she commanded.

"You ain't said nothing but a thing." Puck put his hands on his waist, and with one motion, he yanked his pants and underwear and they fell to the floor. "Umm-hmm, you didn't know old Puck was packing, did you?"

She chuckled, "Yeah, you straight."

"What you laughing for?"

"You got gray hairs on your thang-thang!"

"Well, with age comes wisdom!" Puck shouted. "And it'll be wise if you got naked . . . I ain't got all day; I have to go back to work," he warned.

"Shut the fuck up, gramps!" she said, and lay across the bed and spread her legs wide. "Dinner's ready!"

"Ooooh, that pussy looks wet and juicy. But I don't know where that pussy has been. You gets no licky-licky before the sticky-sticky. That pussy ain't Puck's old friend.

"So bend that fat ass over and remove all of the covers, because my dick is hard like a brick. Don't say shit and keep your big mouth shut, unless you gonna suck on Puck's dick," he rapped, as he threw his hands in the air, and waved them like he just didn't care!

Seven sprung from the bed in rage. "Puck you!" she spat.

"That's my name! Don't wear it out, and it is hard to yell when Puck's dick in your moouuth!" he rapped.

"You gets no sticky-sticky without the licky-licky, Mr. Old School!" she sang.

"I see where this is going!" Puck said.

*Smack-smack!*

"Puck's a Pimp!" he shouted as loud as he could. You don't deserve this dick! Now grovel, cunt!" he said.

Whimpering sounds like a beaten pup came from Seven. The double smack excited Puck, his dick hardened from the adrenaline rush.

"I am gonna take this dick home," he warned.

"No, daddy, no! Please stay. I won't be disobedient again, I promise," she pleaded.

Seven fell to her knees in front of Puck, holding on to his legs so that he wouldn't walk out of the door. Begging for forgiveness, she said to him, "I will do anything. Just don't leave me."

Seven began to give Puck a BJ. Puck didn't complain a bit.

"Does that feel good, big daddy?"

Puck was silent.

"Is it good to you?" she asked.

Again, Puck was silent. He just stood there with his hands on his hips as she took him in.

Raising his penis slightly above her head, she washed his balls with her tongue.

*Smack-smack!* He slapped her lightly on her hand, and then snatched his dick from Seven's hand.

"Did I say you could lick my balls? Huh, cunt? Go get my shit!" Puck pointed to his clothes on the floor. "Get up, bitch, and get my clothes!" he yelled.

"No, daddy . . . I'll be good. Please don't leave me." Seven begged like her life depended on Puck's dick. She hugged Puck's legs so he couldn't leave. "Please, Puck-Puck, I want you, baby." She kissed him gently on his dick and began to suck it with more passion than she had ever mustered with any man.

Puck stood relaxed as she tugged at his penis with her mouth.

"Stop! Stop!" Puck yelled.

"What is the matter?" she asked, while at his mercy.

"Puck likes when it's sucked from the back," he explained.

## Kubuki Love

Puck climbed onto the bed on all fours, and Seven went to work. It felt so good to Puck that his arms collapsed! He landed face down and ass up. He fought every urge to move his hips in a circular motion.

"Oh yeah! Puck likes that shit right there . . . Oh yeah!"

Seven went for broke when she journeyed up to the toss salad shop.

"Oh, got damn!" Puck didn't know she got down like that. But he liked it when she licked it from the back. "Slow motion with it, slow motion with it!" he sang!

Seven didn't let Puck's silly antics break her stride. She is a pro!

"Stop! Stop! Stop-Stop! Stop! Puck's liking it too much . . . I'm a man, you cunt! And a man wants pussy! Lay your ass over here!" He pointed to the bed. "PUCK'S HOUSE! Say what? This is where the magic happens!" he chanted.

Puck rubbed her vaginal lips with the head of his penis until she was wetting internally. Inward, just a little, he pushed it . . . out, he pulls it. Slowly, he put in a little more, then out again. In again, but this time as he held it, he slowly stirred the pussy juices like a pot of magic potion. He continued stirring as he pushed it in and out, like he was drilling.

Seven could feel her body heating up within. She felt herself begin to perspire slightly. Puck got in a full stroke and Seven gasped. Slowly he worked he penis as it rubbed the walls of her love tunnel. As soon as the pussy was in full acceptance of his dick, he yanked out. Seven let out a scream.

With a little force, Puck pulled Seven to the end of the bed. He put her in a the position that he called

"Deep South." But when he said it, it came out sounding like "DEEEE-SOUFFF!"

With her knees in her chest and her pussy barely hanging off of the bed, Puck stood, thrusting and bucking like a jockey.

"Oh, shit!" Seven felt the pressure from his dick, which was wearing her like a glove, filling every inch of her, allowing no air to escape. Their skin slapped together as his pace quickened. He gyrated to the great feeling that was becoming overwhelming.

"DEEEE-SOUFFF!" he yelled as he pounded harder and harder!

Seven was in heaven. She experienced an extended orgasm. She put her hands out, trying to stop old man Puck's stroke.

"DEEEE-SOUFFF!" He pounded.

"Puck is setting it off in this muthafucka!"

His balls slapped against her butt. He got his dick to go in a little further  every time he yelled the words "Deep South." But then she stopped, and Puck was left standing there with his hand clutching the base of his dick. Seven was more than sexually satisfied. Puck grabbed her by her hair and pulled her over to him, where he held his dick.

"Open your mouth, cunt!"

Seven obliged by sucking. Puck released his hold and cum shot out like a pneumatic nail gun shooting nails.

"Drink, cunt! Yeah . . . all of it."

"Ummm," Seven moaned.

Puck was exhausted; he dove into the bed. Seven cuddled beneath him like a helpless child. She held his penis in her hand and she gently kissed his chest.

## *Kubuki Love*

She turned her head upward and kissed his neck; then she continued her climb toward his lips.

"Stop! Stop! Double stop! Bitch, Puck don't recycle! As a matter of fact, get the fuck off of me. I don't love them hoes! Puck gotta go to work! Next time I might make you pay me!"

"Pay?" Seven questioned.

"Yeah! Good dick costs!"

"No buck equals no Puck—No Puck equals no fuck!"

"Oh yeah, one more thing: have some iced tea here for next time, yah-hear? I love it when you call me Big Puck-Puck!" he sang as he left.

## Seven's Haven

Seven met me at the door with only royal blue high heels on. I couldn't help but to stare! Her lips were glossy. I stood there, speechless. She reached forward and pulled me into the house. She led me into the downstairs master bedroom; I licked my lips as I watch her ass cheeks shake like Jell-O. She moved through the house with a feminine glide and the smell of her sweet perfume, invaded my nasal passage.

I figured that this day was the luckiest of my life. My palms became sweat filled, my heartbeat quickened! I could feel the rush of blood to the head of my penis as it hardened! My scrotum tingled! I was so excited, I wanted to rip off my clothes and get it on! I had to keep a cool head about myself and let whatever was going to happen, happen.

She looked over her shoulder at me, then down toward my penis, noticing that it had grown into a medium large-size treat. She smiled as if she had it like that—and she did! Seven knows she is fine as hell.

Into the room and through to the bathroom she took me. There was a flat-screen television playing muted sex recordings, mounted on the wall next to the jetted tub. The tub was filled with water and soft music played, setting the mood. She turned the shower on, that was separate from the tub, and slowly undressed me until the temperature of the shower was to her liking.

I stepped into the shower and began to dance to the scolding hot water that ran quickly down the small of my back. She chuckled as if it was one of the funniest things she had ever seen. She said, "It is not that

144

hot." Then smiled at me with another chuckle hidden beneath her smile.

Stepping into the shower with me, her breasts touched my chest. Her hands grabbed the washrag from behind me, which hung from a shower caddy. The lather thickened, as did my desire to shove my penis into her sexy love pocket. I closed my eyes; the softness of the soapy cloth cuddled my body.

"Why doesn't it feel this good when I do it?" I asked myself. That was a question I could not answer. Maybe it had something to do with me knowing where my hand was going, and not knowing what was in store for me as her hand journeyed across my skin. It was sensuous! I relaxed as she washed my penis, gently sucking my erect nipple. I was so relaxed that when she turned me around and shoved that rag in my ass, I nearly fell out of the shower!

"Bend over!" she requested.

I did. She dug between the only groove in my stank tank.

*Swack!* She smacked my ass. My eyes bucked from the shock. Being slapped on a wet ass was not as pleasant for me as it seems it would be to her. After she washed me, she led me into the jetted tub. At this point, the foreplay session for me was over. I was ready to start fucking! "Patience" is what I kept telling myself.

Noticing my penis was beginning to grow flaccid, she teased it by kissing it gently; then indicated entry with a little tongue, but not enough to take it into her mouth—no, just a little bit of tongue protruded from her lips as she moved about from side to side. The slivering, snake-like motion coached my excitement into producing a rock solid pecker, and it was staring into her eyes like "now what?"

"Bend over!"

I'm thinking *what is with all of the bending over and shit?* But I just went along with it. What the hell?

With cupped hands, she drizzled the water down the crack of my ass. The water was silky, like she had put some type of bath beads into it. She watched in amazement as the water raced like the falls of Niagara. The feeling was explosive when she pulled my dick beneath my legs and began to lick and suck, taking in all that would fit.

Once again I closed my eyes, feeling the ecstasy of it all, when she stopped sucking to lick my ass. Wow! That will make me cum all by itself! Back and forth, she was working her tongue—dick, ass, dick, ass, back to dick, then to ass again. The feeling was confusing!

I came to the conclusion, she will not meet mom! Maybe my dad—but not my mom!

She must have been fiddling with the soap, because her finger slid in my asshole far too easily! My hard dick slapped the tubs water—in and out went her finger. I can't lie, that shit felt good. I moaned like a bitch! She slowly pushed it in and slowly pulled it out. Her other hand massaged my dick as it dangled in the water.

*Swack!*

*I wish she would stop that shit!* I thought.

"Get your bitch ass up and go to the bed!" she spat with anger.

*Oh, this bitch is taking this shit too far!* I thought.

"Getcho ass over there now!" she commanded.

*Swack!* "You ain't moving fast enough!" she yelled.

## Kubuki Love

I captured my dick into the palm of my hand and hustled over to the bed like a green soldier at boot camp. I can say that she was doing her thang so well, that I wasn't about to leave. But if this bitch smacked my ass like that one more time, I was leaving. But only after I get that pussy first!

Over at the bed she laid with her legs spread wide, her finger signaling for me to come near. I got on top of her in a push-up position and she clutched my penis and rubbed the walls of her vagina. It moistened. The warm wetness was delightful; a pleasant aroma escaped her thighs. She wanted it.

I pushed, trying to enter her, but she would not let me in. She just rubbed the outer walls with my dick. Her moans made me want to rape her to get that pussy. I pushed again, and still no luck! She worked it into the pussy about a quarter of the way, then back out again, circling her walls. I was getting anxious for her warm, wet, exhilarating love.

Damn! I'm feeling the need to burst! I wanted to penetrate, but she had me where I couldn't, unless I wanted to lose a limb. My dick was as hard as a bag of marbles; I'm trying to fuck and she is only letting me get the tip of it in.

Alas, she allowed a bit more than just the head of my penis to enter. It went in with ease. I began to stroke that cat with a gyrated motion. She moaned as she pulled my dick out of her mid-stroke! The force behind the thrust caused my penis to bend when it hit the sidewall. She circled the vagina walls that seemed not to want a good, hard dick to invade its comfort zone.

This shit was getting monotonous. Fuck this! I am about to get the fuck outta here and go home with

147

blue balls! As I rose from my mounted position, she clinched my penis harder and looked at me with a look of "oh no, he didn't just try to get up and leave!"

"Where are you going?" she asked with a bit of concern, matched with attitude. "I know you ain't getting up like you're going somewhere? Get yo bitch ass back to your business!" she yelled.

I was shocked. I spat in return, "Fuck you, bitch! I didn't sign up for this shit!"

Yelling loudly, she said, "I said NOW!"

She twisted the once hardened penis she held; she pulled it closely to her even wetter pussy. I raised my hand to smack the shit out of her, but she had pulled me in close enough to thump my nut sack. Damn, that hurt! She was in control at that point.

"Do that shit again I and you will not ever have to worry about this pussy again—EVER!"

I lowered the hand that I was about to slap this bitch with, because one thing a man never wants to do, is mess up with some good pussy.

"Now, like I said, get back to your business, punk ass!" she lectured.

"Look, Seven, if I am to give you dick, you are going to respect it, because frankly, I am beginning to take offense to all of the verbal abuse, ass smacking, and not to mention, the fact that you won't give me no ass!"

She paid my words no attention. She just went back to rubbing her walls with my manhood. She was really getting into this role-playing, or whatever the fuck it is she was doing!

I couldn't take it anymore, so I snatched her hand off my penis and rammed it in with aggression. "Ahh," she sighed. I got off about three good pumps before she shoved me off of her. "You sorry excuse for a good lay! PUT YOUR CLOTHES ON AND GET THE FUCK OUT! NOW, MUTHAFUCKA!"

I couldn't put my clothes on fast enough. I wanted to leave, anyway! I hurried and put my clothes on.

"Fine. I am leaving, Seven! This is bullshit! Your pussy stinks, anyway!"

I turned and began to walk to the door quickly. She tripped me and she came from nowhere with a belt across my ass; then my back. I squirmed with every blow. She beat the shit outta me. I heard her say as she swung that leather with force, "If you ever talk to me like that again, I will beat your punk ass! Now get your bitch ass back in that room and assume the position!"

Feeling that belt made me weep like a child; so I gathered myself and went into the room as I was told. I guess I needed a good cry.

Feeling just a bit insecure, I held my penis with both hands and waited for further instruction from my new dominatrix.

"Assume the position!" she yelled.

"What position?"

"You getting smart?" she asked.

"No!" I replied.

"Well, get on that bed and lay on your back!"

She strengthened me by given me some of the best head this man's dick has ever witnessed. It was out of this world. I felt like letting out another cry. Then she climbed on top of me and rode me while playing with my sack. I could feel my sack relaxing, losing up its shriveled hold. The feeling was amazing! My climax was near until she smacked the shit out of me, again.

"I know you ain't about to cum!" she said with gritted teeth. I can't lie, that smack, coupled with the words, excited me to the point of ejaculation. "I know you ain't about to . . ." *Smack!* "You punk ass bitch!"

She dismounted and grabbed hold of my penis before a drop could exit. She squeezed tightly. Secretions built up within its cylinder. When she released her grip it shot from its base toward the sky. Like a rocket it shot. The release of that pressure was delightful. As it shot toward the sky she thumped my ball sack and followed with a playful massage of them both. The feeling was one that I had never hoped to experience again; although, it was different and pleasure filled. I drifted asleep.

I awoke later that evening tied to the bedpost smelling some god-awful smell. *What the fuck?* was the only thing going through my mind at that time. My body smelled of urine and defecation. I could only gag from the stench. This bitch had peed on me and smeared shit across my stomach! She'd used industrial strength tie straps to attach me to the bed.

She returned to the room with two warmed rags and began to wipe free the waste from my body. "Punk ass!" she yelled. "I see you up. You ready for some more?" she asked.

With my nipples between her fingers of torture, she toyed with them before pinching them a bit harder, until she heard me say, "Ouch! Damn! Why are you so rough?"

"Because you like it, punk ass!"

"And why are calling me punk ass?"

"Punk ass!" she said again.

With her face she took in the aroma of sex from my genital area, teasing the moment with kisses and licks.

150

## Kubuki Love

I was thinking, damn, here we go again. Maybe I picked the wrong day of the week to see her. Out from nowhere she sprayed my balls lightly with perfume. The light mist was cool yet refreshing. Of course, I was like, "What the fuck is she going to do next?"

She leaped from the bed and grabbed a jar from the nightstand. It looked like a science project of some sort. I saw a branch in the jar with some things flying about. "What is that?" I asked.

She just mumbled, "Punk ass!"

The lid came off and she placed the jar's mouth around my balls. I felt several undersized bites. I leaned forward to see what was going on, and found that she had placed mosquitoes in a jar and placed it over my balls. They were biting me. It began to itch and I wanted to scratch them badly.

"How the fuck is that sexy?" I asked myself. The hairs were like walk boards to blood mountains—the infamous mosquito resort. My ankles were tied to a rope attached to a pulley above the headboard. She raised the pulley chain to bring my ankles above my head, after she removed the jar.

"Seven, what are you doing?"

"You better bend your legs so they don't snap," she warned.

Then she placed ass beads in inside me. I tightened up so she couldn't get them in, but she thumped my balls again. A good ball thumping takes your mind away from squeezing your asshole muscles. But she seemed to know her way around, putting those ass beads into my ass.

My mind was focused on counting how many she had inserted: three, four, five. I was feeling like I was going to blackout from the fretfulness of her pulling them back out. Licking around the head of my penis, she took it in. First, about half of it, then she increased her descend toward my itching balls. Repeatedly she worked the shaft of pleasure. The slurping noises got me more and more riled. She lapped her tongue across my balls and slowly, she began pulling one of the beads from its chamber. It felt like I was taking a shit—one rabbit turd at a time.

I'm not sure if I liked it or not. All I knew was when I got away from here, I was not coming back. And damn, my balls began to itch something terrible! I began to sweat. I thought this crazy girl had turned the heat up in this bitch!

"Ummm," she moaned. She licked the sweat from my body like a cat drinking milk, only slower. Then she returned to pleasuring me.

*Plop!* There came another bead. Cum began to gush out from my shaft. She grabbed it once again, and yanked the remaining three from my ass as she released my penis from her Kung Fu grip. Cum shot from my dick like a roman candle!

"Ooh," I moaned. "That was great!"

*Smack!*

She lowered the rope that held my legs above my head and released me from the tie straps. I was drained. My legs quivered as I stood to put my clothes on. I stumbled as I walked to the door.

My ass felt discomfort as it embraced the leather seats in my SUV. I put the keys in the ignition and found that my truck would not start. I checked to see if I had left the radio or the lights on. I went back into the house to use her phone, because my cell battery had died.

## Kubuki Love

"I thought you would never return?" she said as she stood there with those high heels on. I didn't know if I should fuck, fight, or flee for my life? I only weighed a buck and a quarter dripping wet.

I have to say she was a beautiful woman. She wore it all: legs, breast, butt—a straight-up knock out! Yet, I had nothing else to give. I was drained, weak, and slightly terrified, due to her dominance. I couldn't move. I stood still, not wanting to make any moves that would trigger her to run after me.

Okay, it is time to man up! Fuck this! I am not scared of this big bitch. "Bring it on with your funky pussy!" I spat.

She laughed. "Punk ass! You know you want this pussy!" She approached me slowly, kissing me gently on the mouth. I returned her passion.

*Swack!* I smacked her ass to see how she liked it. She took it like a champ! I did it again. *Swack!*

"Yes, daddy, hit this ass again!"

*Swack!*

"I like that shit."

*Swack!*

This shit was beginning to get fun.

*Swack-Swack!*

Her peanut butter skin turned red from my slaps. My dick got hard from excitement. I took off my clothes, bent her over the sofa, and began waxing that ass. I grabbed what little hair she had and pulled it while I stroked her from behind. The control thing was feeling fabulous!

"You like when punk ass fucks that pussy, don't you?" I bullied.

"Yes, daddy!" she answered.

"Take this dick, bitch!" I bullied once more.

I grabbed her waist for leverage and pounded that pussy as hard as humanly possible. Rapidly I stroked, beating that ass to a pulp! She was taking it! All five and three eighths inches! I heard the pussy fart a few times, but I didn't care, I kept stroking. Let it be told, the pussy farts when your dick isn't large enough to fill the hole.

"Pull my hair," she requested.

With my pinching fingers, I grabbed as much as possible and pulled.

"Yes! Now hit me!"

I smacked her ass!

"No, punk ass, hit me!"

I smacked her ass harder.

"You, punk ass muthafucka, you better hit me before I turn around and hit you!" she demanded.

I punched that bitch right in her side."

She grunted and yelled, "Hit me again!"

I hit her ass again."

"Harder!" she yelled with authority.

With gritted teeth, I hit that bitch so hard she collapsed on the floor. I stood over her limp body as if I were at a championship bout. With victory in my heart and a hard dick, I asked, "Are you okay?"

Her body twitched with convulsions as she moaned; that told me she wasn't dead. I wanted to dial 9-1-1 and get the paramedics to the scene because she looked pretty bad. She tried to get up, so I helped her to her feet. She was in high spirits!

*What the fuck?* I thought.

Crouching over, holding her side, she said that was the first orgasm she has had in her life.

"Thanks, punk ass!

*Kubuki Love*


## Open Minded

The message on my answering machine was changed to catch his call, and any other important calls, while I was over my girlfriend's house.

"Thank you for calling. Unfortunately, I am unavailable, but I can be reached at four-five-six . . ." The answer machine beeped.

The phone rang. "It is him, girl, I know it."

"Hello," she answered the phone in her office voice. "Yeah, girl, it's him!"

"Hello," my voice was nervous, as if it was the first time I had ever spoken to him; as if he wasn't my ex.

His voice sounded so sweet, just like I remembered. "Hi," he said. "Whatcha doing?"

Although we weren't together, I felt the need accommodate his every request, so I said, "Nothin'."

I felt so warm inside; it was just like old times, when we used to talk on the phone for hours on end. I know I felt like this, what I don't know is why. I couldn't shake this feeling. He was married now and I should respect that; nevertheless, my heart was weakened by this man. I was held captive in his love dungeon!

"My wife asked me to call you," he said.

I was shocked. He and his wife were talking about me! He had told his wife about our sex. He spoke words to her that aroused her curiosity. She wanted to bear witness and partake in my lovemaking. She was bisexual, which I thought was kind of a marital mismatch. You never know, she could have brought out in him what I couldn't!

"My wife asked me to call you and ask if you would do a threesome with us," he said.

"NO!" The words escaped far too fast. My mind hadn't registered the thought of his request.

"Don't say no right now, think about it first; then answer. You know deep down inside you always wanted to try it. So think about it before you answer."

I stuck with my answer and that's when he said the words I had longed to hear, "I love you! Don't you love me?"

My heart yelled "yes," but my words were soft and weakened. "Yes."

"Then do it for me!"

Like a young cat's meow or a dog's whimpering, I answered, "I will think about it." Then I told him I'd call him later.

As soon as I hung up the phone, I knew I was going to do it. I knew who my heart belonged to. I never knew that love could hurt so good!

I wanted to call him right back and confess my love for him, take back what was taken from me, and tell him with the personality of a 50's movie star, "Yes, I'll do it." I just sat in silence for a moment gazing at the ceiling of my best friend's place. No sound or thought could shake me from my daze. I was lost in my world of what if?

He called me the next day to see if I had reached my decision. What he didn't know was that my decision was made when he asked me to do it for him! I told him "yes," and that he could pick me up about 6:30. I was nervous the whole ride. I wanted to back out and say, "Take me the fuck home."

I saw her for the first time. She greeted me with a hug and a gentle kiss on the cheek. Her smile was warming. First impressions to me are everything. At least in this case it was! I thought she was going to be this unattractive female with a lot of piercings. Boy was I wrong! She wore a sundress that highlighted her curves; her hair was black and silky like she was mixed. Her eyes were slim, kind of like the Chinese. Shit, I thought she was mixed with Black and Philippine. But I later found out she was all Black.

I surveyed the room as if I was a kid on my first day at school. Immediately, the warmth of their cozy townhouse took its effect. The fireplace was lit and the soft voice of Brian McKnight was serenading us from a small distance. The fireplace embraced photos of family, both new and old. The large cherry wood entertainment center housed the stereo, as well as photos and collectibles.

She led me over to their soft, burgundy leather sofa. She retrieved a bottle of chilled wine from the icebox, and we talked and drank for what seemed to be hours!

"Are y'all ready?" The moment of truth had arrived! My palms began to sweat and my heart began to skip beats like a rock thrown across a river. I know she could feel that I was not at ease.

The bedroom was upstairs. Their bed wore satin sheets hugged with a handmade crocheted blanket. The soft smell of vanilla and jasmine held my sense of smell hostage. The room was illuminated only by slow burning candles. The mood was set!

She kissed me gently; she was soft and sweet too! Her lips were softer than the smooth tunes that flowed from their stereo. I was enjoying the kiss so much I barely noticed her fingers stroking my pussy. I invited her to show me more; I longed for her touch.

He sat and watched while his wife took me to other levels. He began to undress and stroke himself. His thick dick was already hardened to the point of pre-cum. He began to rub and stroke his shaft with more intensity. His emotional expressions and gestures displayed he was in awe, but he knew not of the pleasure I was experiencing!

She sucked my nipples, one after the other, causing little pimples like dots to appear around them. My nipples were harder than a convict's dick! Her kisses began to descend until she reached the valley of my goodness. She laid me gently on the bed and wasted no time feasting on my pussy. And I wasted no time providing her with the juices she desired. All she needed was a biscuit the way she sopped up my love gravy.

The anticipation was edging him to participate. My eyes closed from the orgasmic pleasures unknown to man. She knew exactly what to do—strategic, precise maneuvering! I was ready to explode again. I did! Her lips kissed mine and I wanted to taste her as she did me. My fingers danced generously between her legs as I sucked her breast. She gyrated slowly with a rhythmic pace. I removed my fingers and sucked her juices from each of them. She helped! *Umm* . . . sweet! My stomach growled for more!

I couldn't wait any longer to satisfy this hunger for her. First, I tried the ABC method, but only made it to G, before giving most of my attention to her clit. I felt him behind me rubbing his dick along the sugar walls of my throbbing pussy. *This* is what I wanted. *This* is what I needed. I had to have him inside of me. I reached back and put him in me. My hand cupped his ball sack and gently caressed them. With all that was going on, it was like patting yourself on the head and rubbing your stomach, while your tongue made circles freely in the air, all at the same time. His grind was delightful! I stopped for a minute and tucked my bottom lip beneath my teeth. His pace quickened!

I could feel his cum trickle down my thighs accompanied by my flow of love. I could taste the sweetness of her explosion as I squeezed the fullness of her breasts. The sex was so intense that we formed a triangle and sucked each other's nectar. Shit, we only had to yell switch once!

Morning fell upon us quickly. I was awakened by her touch! She and I made love again, before he and I showered and left for work. Dayuuum! I never knew it would be so sweet!

Thank you for that experience, baby!

I love you,

4ever yours

## Open Mic Night

Eddie was waiting on Maurice to arrive, but he was late as usual. It was never surprising that he was late. Hell! He was never on time! It was the pretty boy in him, that wouldn't allow him to be prompt.

*Fuck worrying about him. I need to make certain that I looked my best,* Eddie thought. He put his purple velour jacket on over top of his lavender ruffled shirt, and stood in the mirror admiring himself. "Damn, you fine," he said, looking in the mirror as he straightened his jacket so that his ruffles were showing.

Doing the latest dances, he began to brush his shoulders off. With a make believe microphone in his hand, Eddie began to rehearse, but words got in the way and he starting freestyling rhymes.

"Fuck that nigga! Late-ass nigga! Always talking 'bout his dick is bigger. But I figure, fuck that nigga! Begging-ass nigga! Talking about dick when your pockets are thinner!"

Eddie's concentration was broken when heard keys jingling in the door. Maurice didn't get in the door good before Eddie began his interview. "Where you been? Why you late? What took you so long? Why didn't you call?"

Maurice yelled back, "Why you look like Prince?" Then he continued, "And where do you think we are going, the Cherry Moon?"

"Stop making fun of my outfit, Maurice, because that shit isn't funny! Let's go!"

"I really think you should change this hideous entourage of fabric!" Maurice pleaded.

Eddie just looked at him. "Come on!"

## Kubuki Love

"Okay, if you say so. But it is a bad choice of clothing. And I bet you never went out with Nicole looking like the Purple one!"

"Nicole and I is none of your concern, Maurice."

"You didn't say that when I was . . ."

"Watch your mouth!" Eddie warned.

"Yeah, I bet you do!"

"Come on before I lose my cool."

"Who is driving?"

"I'll drive," Eddie answered.

The entire ride Maurice joked on Eddie's clothes.

Eddie drove up to the front of the club and let the valet park the car.

There were a few folks in line, but the line wasn't wrapped around the corner like it is shown to be in movies or videos. Only a few waited patiently for the opportunity to enter the club.

Club Kubuki was never in the same location and it was invitation only! The secret operators of the operation always booked the location one week in advance, which allowed plenty of time to set the erotic atmosphere. One of the three sceneries of the rotating stage was set in purple and accented with gold. Plush velvet cushions and décor put you in the mind of royalty. It was fitting for a king!

Hott Like Fire was performing as Eddie and Maurice made their way to the back of the club where the performers were.

"Damn, you make my pussy sweat!" she moaned; then continued, "Giving me face I won't forget! I am getting your face so soak and wet. Can you taste the fruits of your labor yet? Eat this pussy, baby, or would you rather instead, hold firm my thigh's stern, as I guide your head?

"Yeah, that's what I want! Lick between my ass cheeks, brown like chocolate, so tasty and sweet. Damn, you ass licker, head giver speaking to me in tongue; making my soul quiver!"

"Hey, bubba, has Lazy Back went up yet?" Eddie asked the host of the night.

"Naw! She still back in the purple room getting ready."

"Cool, I am going to go holler at her for a minute. Maurice, I will be back in a minute. I need to kick it with my girl before she goes on," Eddie said.

"Okay, I will be right here just enjoying the show, waiting patiently," Maurice replied sarcastically.

"Stop tripping. I am only going to speak to her. You know we go way back like slave days and whipped backs."

"That shit was corny! Go see your bitch. I'll be right here!" Maurice snapped.

"Is all of that necessary, Reese? I can't take you anywhere," Eddie mumbled.

"Can't nobody take your black ass nowhere, punk ass, befuddled, diminutive maggot!!!" Reese snapped.

Eddy couldn't believe what he'd just said, nor did he know what he just called him; but he knew it didn't sound like it was nice. He just turned and walked away. There wasn't a good comeback for whatever he just called him. *Befuddled?*

"Hey, baby! I haven't seen you in a while, how are you?" Lazy said, sounding surprised to see Eddie.

"I'm good. I just had to come back here to see you before you went on."

"Oh, okay. That's all to the good. So, what you doing later? Maybe we can get together and catch up on old days and time missed."

162

"Okay, let's do that. I just have to rid myself of my friend Maurice."

"Have I met him?"

"No, but he has met you indirectly, because I talk about you all the time."

Lazy just smiled, with a little blushing to boot.

"Hey, why don't you come and meet him real quick?"

"Okay."

The two of them walked back over to where Reese was standing patiently.

"Hey, Reese this Lazy Back."

"What kind of name is Lazy Back?" he asked in a snotty way, as he barely shook her hand.

"Reese, be nice. Lazy got her name from our boy Tom-Tom, because she has a lazy eye and her last name is Bacoria. We used to refer to her as 'Lazy Eye Erica Bacoria.' As we grew older, we just shortened it.

"Coming to the stage we have two newcomers to the KLP stage! Tonight, they call themselves Who GAF. Doing an original piece called: Reese's Penis: The Reality Poetry.

"Who GAF!" the host called again as he waited for the two to come from behind the curtain.

The stage director called out for Who GAF.

"Hey, Eddie, that is us. Say good-bye to Lazy; we have to go!"

"Here we are," Maurice answered back.

"Hey, you guys are on, follow me." He grabbed Maurice's shoulder.

The stage director called to the host in his radio and told him they were on their way to the stage, entering from his right. The host introduced them again as the appeared.

"How are you all doing tonight? Sorry for the delay. We hope you enjoy this original piece. We call this, 'Reality Poetry.' Because it's real-time lyrics being performed. Rappers call it 'coming off the top of the dome' or 'freestyling' if you will. But here it goes.

"Damn . . . I am nervous as fuck! I should be doing a poem about fuckin' this nigga right here in the butt!" He smack Eddie's ass.

"But I think I have a better place to put this nut." Maurice traces Eddie's lips with his finger.

Eddie stands behind Maurice and begins by running his hands down his chest toward his pants. All the while, Maurice continues delivering his poetry. He unzips Maurice's pants and inserts his hand and strokes Maurice's penis.

"Who GAF stands for: *who gives a fuck!* I care not who watches this dick getting sucked!*"

Eddie gently slides Maurice's pants down, and then he pulls Reese's penis from his silk boxers.

"Damn, dude, is this penis looking nice or what? Taste it now, don't wait! Now drop my drawers from around my waist. Lick these balls, how do they taste? But don't look up at me, I can't concentrate. I got to spit this poem as your spit coats my loin, I gyrate."

Eddie slurps and makes a moaning noise.

"Stage help, please bring me a stool and put it beneath my ass, before I lose my footing. This shit is feeling so good, I may lose my cool. I'd fuck around fall and we look like fools, in front of all of y'all watching this skit. Headlines read: A Fine, Black Nigga's Dick Gets Bit. You'll be laughing at my dumb ass until last call and shit!"

Maurice laughs as he says, "Talking about, did you see that dude fall while dude was sucking his dick?

# Kubuki Love

And he didn't even stop, he just kept to it, sucking and slobbering all over that dick! Thanks, stage hand, for getting this seat. Now I can enjoy him, enjoying my meat.

"The sensation is near, I feel its tingle. Damn, this feels good. It's so good to be single! Without my thrusting, I feel a pushing. Toward the head of my shaft it is rushing. You may ask if something is wrong. The Jamaican in me says, 'Nuttin'; the crème filling seems to be gushing!

"That feels good. Now clean it well and don't leave anything! Swallow it down. Now you are full of what you have been wanting! And our audience who has taken in the sight, I thank you for cumming to open mic night."

Applause burst from the crowd as the MC was handed the mic.

"Oh,. . . my . . . goodness. I mean CUM on! He swallowed it. Give it up for Maurice and Eddie. Better known as MO Easy! With that stunning piece—what do you call that, Reese's Penis?"

"Yeah! It is our new and original style called Reality Poetry!" Maurice shot back.

Acknowledging Maurice, the MC said, "Cool, here at the KLP for the first time re-al-it-y poetry!! Next coming to the stage is Lazy Back!"

"I was nervous, Eddie. What about you?"

"Fuck you, bitch!"

"What are you so mad about?"

"I told your bitch ass, I didn't want you to cum in my mouth! Your cum tastes like cow snot!"

"What about you? Your balls be smelling like moisture damage!"

"Fuck you! We weren't even supposed to do that one. We were supposed to do my piece!" Eddie said.

"Fuck you!" Reese spat back.

"Take me home!" Eddie yelled.

"Walk, bitch!" Reese yelled back.

"Wait a minute? I drove! You walk, bitch!"

"Fine! I will call a cab, you fat maggot!"

"Fat maggot! Who in the fuck are you calling a fat maggot?"

"You muthafucka! With your fat-ass girlfriend! I don't see what Nicole sees in your broke, trifling ass, anyway. You thug wannabe! She needs to leave your silly ass alone."

"Eddie, where you going?" Reese asked as Eddie just turned and walked away.

Eddie handed the valet the ticket for his vehicle. Eddie had nothing else to say as he entered his car. Reese jumped in the passenger side.

"Hey, man, I am sorry. I should have never went there."

*Whap!* Eddie backhanded Reese. "And don't you ever go there again!"

Reese crouched over holding his face. "What you do that for?" Coming up with a backhand of his own, catching Eddie off guard. *Whap!*

Wrong thing to do; all Eddie saw was stars. Those stars became flashing lights and questions.

"Sir, can you hear me? What is your name? Can you tell me what happened?" Officer Mattayo asked.

Dazed, Eddie wasn't sure what just happened. He didn't even remember being in the car.

"Sir, have you been drinking? Your friend is being airlifted to the hospital. What is his name?"

"Who?"

"The passenger, sir?"

"What passenger?"

"Excuse me, sir. We must get him to the hospital immediately. He has suffered multiple rib breakage and a damaged breast plate," the medic informed the officer.

"Okay," the officer agreed, before jumping in the ambulance with Eddie.

"Officer Mattayo, you cannot ride back here. We need room to work," the attendant said.

Officer Mattayo hopped out of the ambulance.

"Okay, sir. I am going to need you to open your eyes! The nurse tapped him slightly on the left side of his forehead. Come on stay with us . . . open them eyes! Tell me your name?"

"Edward Shaw," he said weakly. "Edward Shaw," he repeated slowly, all the while licking his blood drenched lips.

"And how old are you, Mr. Shaw?"

"Seventeen."

"I am sorry, Mr. Shaw, I am not buying that one; maybe some years ago. So, why don't you tell me your real age?"

Ummm-ummm, I-ummm, I, ummm, I . . . t-t-t-t—" Eddie started shaking and having convulsions.

Later . . .

Eddie turned and looked toward the door from his hospital bed and noticed that Nicole being wheeled by.

For more about Eddie, please purchase *Ain't Nothing Like Big Girl Lovin'* by Jau'wel.

## 30-Day Guarantee

"I can't believe Judith's ass; always running her damn mouth to Gerald. Every time I turn around she is all up in his face, telling all my business! She got some damn nerve with her pink ass. I ought to whoop her ass one good time. Ol' pink bitch!" complained Evelyn.

"Oh, hi, Mr. Gerald," Samantha and Evelyn sang together.

"Hello, Sam. Hi, Evelyn. How are you?" David Gerald replied.

Evelyn thought he wanted to ask why she was late coming to work today. "I know that pink bitch told him I was running late," she mumbled under her breath.

"I am fine, Mr. Gerald. Just got small issues at home with the old man."

"Just make sure you take care of them so that you're not late again, Evelyn."

"Sure, Mr. Gerald," Evelyn responded as Mr. Gerald continued to his office.

"OH, I knew that bitch snitched on me. I should tell her husband that she is sucking his dick at lunchtime."

"What, girl?" Samantha asked.

"Yeah, that's why he hasn't fired me yet, because he knows I know. I ought to put both their asses on blast and tell his wife!"

"Girl, you are too silly. You wouldn't do that." Sam laughed.

"Yes, I would! She should know that her husband is cheating on her with that pink bitch behind her back, because she stopped sucking his dick six years ago."

"Girl, whatchasay? I know that's right!" Samantha said and then she continued, "So how you know that much about the Gerald's?"

"Because I caught them together one night they thought they were alone."

"They got busy here?" Sam asked.

"Yeah, girl, let me tell you what happened. That pink bitch figured everyone had left for the night, but she didn't check the restrooms. I was in the stall going for broke and, girl, did I have that bathroom on fire! I gathered myself and washed my hands when . . ."

"Girl, get to the damn point!" Samantha interrupted.

"Okay, okay—so, as I came out the bathroom I heard noises that sounded like slurping and moaning. I stopped dead in my tracks! I listened . . . 'Oh shit, that's it! Yeah, I like that.' I snooped and peeked until I saw the whole thing going down. Girl, I sat there and watched the whole thing."

"No, you didn't?" Sam spat.

"Yes, I did! I wanted to see what he was working with."

"They didn't see you?"

"No. I had ducked down. And besides, they were too into themselves at the moment."

"Then what?"

"I have to say Judy got skills! She was taking all two inches to the head like a champ! I never have seen anyone who could give head movement in such a quick, but short, fashion. I mean she looked like this." Evelyn gave a quick illustration of what Judith had done while giving head.

Laughter rained throughout the office as Samantha found that to be the funniest thing she has ever heard.

"His dick is only two inches? Damn, no wonder his family calls him peewee!" Sam laughed.

"Girl, look . . . and then, guess what?"

"What?" Sam questioned.

"He went and laid his little-dick ass in the chair and she started licking everything in her sight."

"She nasty!"

"Yeah, that bitch is nasty. Mr. Gerald told her that it had been a long time since he had that done to him. And she asked how long. He replied six years. But he's been married for nine years, so you know . . ."

"Call Mrs. Gerald, right now, and tell on peewee!" Samantha told Evelyn.

"Naw, I am going to wait until the time is right. I need to keep my trump card available."

Judith

"Hey, Mom, how are you feeling today?"

"Baby, I am feeling weak, but I'll be all right."

"Mom, have you made another appointment?"

"Yeah, baby. I go to the doctor's today at two."

"Do you have anybody to take you?"

"No."

"Then how were you going to get there?"

"The bus."

"The bus, Ma? I can't let you take the bus. I will take you."

"Okay, Judy., I am going to hang up now. I have to take my medication and rest a bit. I will be ready to go when you get here. Remember, I have to be there at two."

"I will be there, Ma. I am going to let you go; I have a call coming in okay?"

"Okay, baby, see you later."

"Hello?"

"Hey, Judy, how are you? This is David Gerald. I want to see you, if you're not too busy."

"Sorry, Mr. Gerald."

"David, please," he interrupted.

"David, I have to take my mother to the doctor's office by two."

"So that means you have at least four hours to kill, right?"

"I guess you can say that."

"Well, may I come over?"

"Where is your wife?"

"She is shopping."

"For how long?"

"What's with all the questions?"

"What, I can't ask questions?"

"Not those questions! Geez, Judith, you sound like a cop!"

"Well then, why do you want to see me if I'm a cop?"

"You are twisting my words now; I didn't say you were a cop."

"Well, I went to church Wednesday night and I got saved."

"You got what?"

"Saved!" Judith said clearly.

"Staged? What is that?"

"Saved, David—I said SAVED!" she yelled into the phone.

"Oh . . . saved. Well, that is great!"

"So I don't think I can be with you like that anymore," Judith said softly.

"Anymore than what?"

"Anymore period."

"Wait, wait, wait . . . Don't be like that, Judith. How are you going to change our arrangement without telling me first?"

"Arrangement? Is that what we have? And I am telling you now."

"I am saying it's Friday and you got saved on Wednesday night. We could have seen each other a few more times, and you could have done it on Sunday."

"David, you don't wait to get saved just so you can have sex with a MARRIED MAN!"

"Judith, I'm coming over." He hung up quickly before she could even ask him for what.

David Gerald

David knocked at the door, then calls for her.

"Judith, it's David."

He knocks again. "I'm coming, David," a voice screamed from inside.

The door opened. Judith stood in the doorway, blocking David from entering.

"Yes, David?"

"Are you going to let me in?"

She eased from the door and allowed him to enter. She was wearing a short skirt that fit snug. David couldn't help but look at her ass as he walked by.

"You look good, Judith."

"Thanks, now what do you want?" Judith said, crossing her arms across her chest.

"I want to talk, that's all."

"Talk about what?"

"You pick the subject."

"Okay, let's talk about Jesus."

"Okay, I'll pick the subject then," David smirked as he began to speak. "Come a little closer."

"Why?"

"So we can talk."

"Why do I have to be close?"

"So I won't have to raise my voice, and besides, you can hear me better."

"Yeah right, don't try anything."

"I won't. Just come closer. You look nice today."

"You said that already."

"Okay, Okay. I just wanted to be with you today. I miss you."

"Be with me how? I told you I'm a saved woman and we can no longer see each other."

"Okay, one more time and I promise, I will not pursue you anymore."

David persisted to pour on the charm with Judith, trying everything in the book. He was slowly wearing her down. The more he talked, the weaker she got.

"Come on, baby," he whispered, as he nibbled at her ear and then began kissing her neck.

"Oh, David," She moaned, "I am trying to live right."

"Baby, live for the right now, come on, I promise I'll just put the tip in, that's it. Please."

"Just the tip?" she smiled.

"Just the tip," he giggled playfully.

"I don't know, David."

David pulled his penis out and pulled her hand toward it. "See, its wanting you." He rubbed his hard penis with her hands. She was acting as if she didn't want to touch it, but showed no resistance. He continued to polish his penis with the back of her hand.

Feeling that she could not fight the feeling anymore, he tossed his tongue down her throat. She began to stroke his dick without assistance. David began to rub her mound of moisture, feeling how wet he had gotten her, excited him more. He grew a whole half inch larger.

"Damn, baby, this pussy is wet. I want to taste it, may I?"

She couldn't resist the temptation of the flesh. Off came the underwear in an instant, when he offered to lap up here juices. She was so ready! David didn't waste any time indulging. Judith looked down to witness this unforgettable feeling. David went into his pocket and pulled out a pouch. Without missing a drop of her juice, he poured a little of the contests into his mouth. The feeling intensified as she got wetter. She felt little tingling sensations going off like the Fourth of July!!!

*Pop, pop, pop.* The Pop Rocks setoff in David's mouth. Judith held his head while she watched in amazement. *Lord, please forgive me,* was the thought that ran through her head, but this sin was far too enjoyable for her to let pass. "OMG!" Judith shouted. All the while David's face stayed buried, as if he had fallen asleep. He came up for a second to more Pop Rocks into his mouth.

"Damn, you taste so sweet, baby," David said.

Judith buried his face back in the place with both hands, as if she were implying, stop talking with your mouth full. She was exploding inside, and she thought, *How can I feel this way with a married man?*

David lowered his head, brushing her clitoris with his nose, and then raised it with a sweeping motion with his chin. Once that chin went in, it felt like a man's penis, so Judith began to hunch David's chin. Grinding and squeezing, until she squeezed all her juices into his forgiving mouth.

David stood to his feet and pulled down his trousers to reveal his hardened penis—all two inches! But he refused the service of fucking Judith or even getting a BJ.

"I am tired now, David, and I have to get my mother and take her to her doctor's appointment. You are going to have to let your wife finish my job for me, and tell her I said, 'Thanks'."

David looked dumbfounded as he retrieved his clothes and went on his way.

Judith trotted off to the shower so she wouldn't be late picking up her mother.

*I can't believe that bitch did me like that.* David thought as he wiped his mouth as if he'd left a residue.

"I got a trick for her. I am going to pile so much paperwork on her desk for her to do, that she will be begging to give me some of that pussy, just to get out of work."

"Hi, Mr. Gerald."

"Hi, Evelyn, where is Sam today?"

"She had to take her kids to the dentist, remember?"

"Yeah, I remember. Okay, I will be in my office if anyone needs me."

"Yes, sir," Evelyn replied.

"Oh . . . oh, can you call Judith? I need to see her in my office."

"Yes, sir," she replied again.

Evelyn picked up the phone and pressed the button that rang to Judith's office.

"Hello, this is Judith Parker, how may I assist you?"

"Mr. Gerald needs to see you in his office."

"Okay. Thanks."

Judith gathered herself as to look as professional as she could while in the work place. She walked down the hall and into his office with confidence.

"Yes, Mr. Gerald?"

"Come on in, please. Close the door and have a seat, Ms. Parker."

"Yes, sir."

Once the door was closed, Mr. Gerald could speak what was on his mind. "Judith, what was that shit Friday? And then you didn't even call Saturday or Sunday."

"I went to church Sunday and I was with my mom on Saturday."

"So, did you do it?"

"Do what?"

"Get saved again."

"I got saved Wednesday, David."

"So, we all good, right?"

"No! I repented Sunday and asked God to forgive me for all my sins, including the one we committed."

"But I am trying to finish what we started Friday."

"Oh, we finished! Why don't you get Mrs. Gerald to suck your little dick?" she said.

David was surprised that Judith called his dick little.

"Little?" he spat.

"Yeah, little. Why don't you get her to give you sex?"

"You know I haven't gotten a BJ from my wife in six years, I told you that. We only have sex once a month. You know a man can't live off of that. So I told her plenty of times in our marriage that our sex life needed improvement, and she still hasn't changed, so I gave it thirty days after we discussed it from the last time, before I guaranteed myself that I would seek satisfaction from someone else."

"Ya'll need counseling and you need Jesus!" Judith said. "So, are we finished, Mr. Gerald? Because I have a lot of paperwork to do. Thank you."

"Have a good day, Ms. Parker."

Evelyn called up Samantha on the phone.

"Oh, girl, look . . . Mr. Gerald called Judy into his office and they been in there for about thirty minutes."

"What are they talking about?" Samantha asked.

"I don't know, but I know she had a lot of paperwork on her desk this morning. And she came out of his office mumbling something about thirty days and a guarantee."

"Girl, you supposed to get the whole scoop," Samantha commented.

"What am I supposed to do, put my ear and a glass to the door?"

"I'll ask Bernard later. I know he will get the real story because he and Judith is playing pool tonight at that pool hall on Sewell's Point Road."

"Are you going?" Samantha asked.

"No. I don't hang out at that hole in the wall."

"Don't you like Bernard?"

"Girl, no, his breath be smelling like pet milk all the time. But his boy, Jay, is looking good these days."

"Jay'rone?" Samantha asked.

"Yes, girl, he is fine!"

"That is my cousin's cousin, Man-Man, on their mamma's side. I can hook you up."

"I don't know, Sam."

"Come on, girl, I'll bring CJ and we can double!"

"Okay."

"Let me call Man-Man and hook it all up, and I will call you back later."

"Cool."

*Kubuki Love*

## Torpedo Sammie

A pair of candy-blue pants, red shirt, yellow tie, a yellow belt with green boots and pink socks, is what she made Sammie wear while she shopped. She had won the bet. He felt like a walking disco light as he paraded throughout the stores. Yeah, she got him good, but a deal was a deal.

She told him she had to bring his arrogance to a halt. She implied: "SAMMIE thinks he is all that. SAMMIE thinks he has it going on! SAMMIE only worries about SAMMIE."

So, the NBA game was coming on and she bet him that the team he chose would lose against the one she chose. Sammie had first choice and he knew that he'd never lose. Well, guess what? Double overtime, final seconds . . . the crowd counted down as the ball was inbounded. "Ten, nine, eight . . ." The shot was pulled to win the game. "Six, five, four . . ." The three is buried with 1.6 seconds left. The crowd was outraged!

"Oh my God!" he shouted. "Did you see that?"

Sammie's mouth dropped to the floor; the game was finally over, until the opposing team inbounded half court to the star player with 1.6 seconds left. He knew it was nearly impossible at this point for them to win the game. They needed four points for the win! The inbound pass touched his fingers for six seconds. In the remaining second, the crowd watched the ball hit nothing but net! The whistle blew as the buzzer sounded.

Foul on number fourteen. One shot, the referee signaled. The fans were starting toward their cars; others stood and watched as he sank the free throw.

"Yeah, boyee! I told you!" Gayle yelled, as she pumped her fist in excitement. "Woo-whoo!" She laughed. "Time to pay up!" Gayle advised.

He knew it was time to pay the piper. That was when she told him her plan to bring him down a notch. He was a team player, so it was cool.

There were two kids in particular that followed Sammie around the mall pointing and giggling. One of them had the nerve to call him gumdrop. He couldn't rid himself of this fat kid and his bucktooth buddy. He wanted to tell them a thing or two. *Ole fat bastard!* But anyway, he had a chance to redeem himself and he was going to take advantage of the opportunity.

"What are you watching?" Gayle inquired.

Sammie was hesitant to answer, but he said, "This dumb-ass game show."

"So, what's coming on next?" she asked.

He pressed the Guide button on the remote and then answered, "Another dumb-ass game show."

"Do you care to make another bet?"

"Why? What are you going to make me wear, a dress next?"

"No, I don't have plans to make you wear a dress."

"So, what is the bet?" he asked.

"The same as before: we have to do whatever the winner has for us to do."

"Okay, bet," he immediately responded.

The game show was about two families battling for points gained from their answers, against what the survey said.

"I got the Johnson family!"

"I'll take the Talley family," she came back with.

Let's say in short, that I didn't win that one, either.

## Kubuki Love

Gayle gloated as she concocted her new plan for Sammie.

When Sammie got home, there was an index card attached to the door that read: BE AT THIS ADDRESS AT 7PM, WEARING THE OUTFIT I LEFT FOR YOU IN YOUR ROOM. PLEASE BE ON TIME! A BET IS A BET! GAYLE.

Inside the room was a box with a card attached. It read: PUT THIS OUTFIT ON AND GO PICK UP MY GRAND-MOTHER'S BIRTHDAY CAKE. ACROSS THE STREET FROM THE CAKE PLACE IS A FLOWER SHOP. GET A DOZEN LILIES. SHE LOVES THEM. I HAVE ALREADY CALLED THE ORDER IN, SO EVE-RYTHING SHOULD BE READY. SEE YAH AT 7. GAYLE.

Sammie did as the letters instructed. The box contained a costume. Kind of like the one Huggie-Bear wore in *I'm Going to Get You Sucker*, but without the fishbowl shoes.

"I ain't wearing this fucking jumpsuit! She's crazy as hell! You know what? Fuck it. I am going to wear it, but I got a trick for her ass!"

Grandma Tartuffe had her best dress on and was with seven of her friends, helping her to bring in her 75th birthday. Sammie arrived on time as he was told, dressed in a pimped-out jumpsuit. As soon as he entered the party, Gayle signaled the DJ to play the music from the *Super Fly* soundtrack. She yelled, "Surprise, Grandma, the entertainment is here!"

The music played. He began to search his immediate surroundings trying to find "the entertainment," as she put it. He noticed that all eyes were on him! He found it disgusting that a room full of women, old enough to date Moses, were screaming, "Take it off— Take it off!"

He turned to leave because this was some bullshit! "I am not dancing for these old-ass ladies!" he mumbled.

"Are you backing out on the debt you owe me?" Gayle asked.

"No."

"Well"—*Smack!* Gayle hit Sammie on his bottom—"come on, Supa Fly. Shake something!"

Sammie began to wind his waist toward Grandma like he really didn't want to do it, but that is what he got for betting. All of the ladies were screaming, "Supa Fly!" Sammie stripped down to his drawers as he danced for the excited women.

Grandma was way too excited that Supa Fly was waving his goods in her face. Grandma took out her teeth and softly bit his penis as he dangled it close to her lips. That made a near hardened penis into a stiff one. Sammie actually had thoughts of getting with Grandma after that stunt. Grandma was a freak and she liked this shit. Grandma rubbed the dollar from the back of his balls to the rim of his tight-ass drawers, copping a feel the whole way. Jostling the dollar into his drawers she pulled the fabric away from his skin far enough to catch a peek.

"Okay, I am done!" Sammie said, as he turned to leave.

Gayle laughed hard at her grandma's antics. "You can stop, you paid your debt," she giggled.

She kissed his lips and told Sammie that she would see him later after the party was over. Sammie put his clothes on a left immediately.

It was two AM and Gayle hadn't shown. At three AM, still no Gayle. Finally Sammie went to sleep.

## Kubuki Love

The next morning Gayle had some lame-ass excuse why she didn't make it. Sammie was upset about dancing for granny, but denied the fact that he enjoyed the attention. He also didn't like the fact that Gayle didn't show up, so he could get his freak on.

Sammie began to question Gayle as she walked through the door at 11:28 AM, two days later.

"Gayle, where have you been? I waited all night for you and you haven't called me in two days," Sammie questioned.

"I was with Grandma; she got drunk and started hitting on the DJ."

Sammie started laughing. "Your granny is a freak."

"But wait, the DJ got with her after all of her friends left. I was crashed out on the couch and I woke from my sleep when I heard some moaning coming from the kitchen. I got up to investigate and I noticed my grandma's teeth on the counter. The DJ had his bare ass on top of the counter and Grandma was giving him head.

"I didn't say shit. I just stood and watched. She deserved to get it on if she could. I couldn't hate. But guess what? They didn't stop once they noticed I was standing there. He continued getting his dick sucked by my grandma. I went back to the couch. I couldn't take it anymore. I couldn't sleep because he had Grandma moaning while he was hitting it."

"He hit it, too?" Sammie asked with a smile on his face.

"Yeah," Gayle responded.

"How you know if you went back to the couch?" he asked.

"I could hear their skin slapping, that's how," she said.

"Umph, that's a shame; seventy-five and still getting her freak on!" Sammie reminded her.

"I had to take her to the doctor this morning. I guess the sex was too much for her and had drained her physically. She has been sleeping ever since."

Tears ran down Sammie's face as he laughed.

"So, you want to lose anymore bets?" Gayle questioned.

"Yeah, sure, I'll bet you," he said.

"What is the wager this time?" he asked.

"Same as before," she said.

"Let's just flip a coin; best out of three."

"Okay, flip! And we'll call it in the air."

Sammie pulled a quarter out of his pocket and tossed it high in the air. "Heads."

"Let it hit the ground—let it hit the ground!" Gayle shouted.

The coin hit the ground and rolled under the couch. Sammie pushed the couch out of the way. "Tails!"

"Ha!" Gayle cheered. "Toss it again!"

Sammie tossed the coin into the air again.

"Heads!" he yelled a second time. It landed on heads.

"Okay, we are tied and the winner gets to choose first," Sammie said.

The coin goes high into the air for the third time. "Heads!" he yelled.

The coin didn't even roll; it landed flat on the ground displaying heads.

Sammie tightened his fist and made a muscle. "Yes! I won.

"Okay, Gayle, this is what it is. I am going to flip this coin again, and if it lands on heads, you have to give me just that—head.

"And if it lands on tails?" Gayle's eyebrows rose.

"Then I get to put it in your tail." Sammie smiles.

"Oh, hell no!" she said.

Gayle asks with great concern, "You're kidding, right?"

"Sorry, but I'm not.," Sammie smiled.

He tossed the coin before Gayle could respond. The coin hit the ground. "Tails!"

"Yes!" Sammie expressed. "Bring your tail back here at 8 PM, and be sure to use the restroom prior to coming to my Kubuki Love Palace.

"Hold up, player, I didn't say I was going to do that!"

"A bet is a bet. Are you going back on what we agreed?" Sammie asked.

"Flip again, Sammie."

"Fuck no, one-time deal. Okay, eight o'clock, Gayle!" Sammie warned.

Sammie sang to the tune of a famous rap song: "Eight PM, she'll be at my house; nine PM, I'll be busting her out; ten PM, I'm going to cum in her mouth; eleven PM will be just like ten. I am going to fuck her in the ass, until I'm cumming again," Sammie sang, giving himself a high five.

Gayle showed at eight as planned, to pay her debt. Sammie had put desensitizer on the head of his penis, so he could fuck all night. Gayle wanted to stall because she was scared to even think how it would feel to have a dick going in and out of her ass.

"Let's take a shower first," Gayle said.

After the shower, Sammie was ready. He warned her that she must first relax her muscles and just let him work it. They lay across the bed and Gayle agreed to try it. Sammie instructed her to lie in the position to receive. Gayle purposely squeezed her hole closed so it would be hard for Sammie to get it in; then she said, "It won't fit."

"Relax, Gayle," Sammie coached.

"Sammie, this isn't working, so let me just give you some pussy and we can call it even?"

Sammie was clearly disappointed with Gayle.

"Can I get some soft French kisses below?" he asked.

"You know I don't give BJs, Sammie. That is why you came up with this crazy ass bet." She smacked her lips.

"Gayle, when you won, I didn't complain when I had to wear those gay-ass colors while you shopped, or when you made me strip for your ninety-year-old freaky-ass grandma!"

"She is seventy-five, Sammie! And I didn't ask to stick something in your ass or make you suck a dick!"

"So, you backing out?" he asked.

"No."

"Okay, turn your ass over then!"

"Wait, Sammie, let's just fuck, okay?"

"All right, fuck it! That shit ain't right, though. I did that dumb shit you wanted me to do without complaint! You are going give me this pussy right now, again when my dick gets hard again, then again when I wake up," he demanded.

Gayle agreed and told him to put on a condom.

The morning fell upon them quicker than they had assumed. Sammie had bitched so much that Gayle gave him the pussy every time his dick got hard. He got off five good nuts.

"Okay, Sammie, that's enough. I need to rest." Within ten minutes, Gayle was asleep.

Sammie knew it was the right time for pay back. He waited until she was snoring and really deep into her sleep, before he stood over her and released his urine into the condom he was wearing; the semen-filled condom began to saturate with urine quickly. As the condom filled with urine, it slowly began to slide from his shaft. The weight of the warmed mixture of early morning cum and hot piss came crashing toward the bridge of Gayle's nose. Shocked out of her sleep, she smelled of urine, sex, and morning breath.

"What the fuck?" She just cried on the spot. "Why did you do that?" she asked.

"Because you went back on your word; we are over! Now get the fuck out, 'cause you have just been hit by Torpedo Sammie, bitch!"

## Oscar Charlie Delta

Herman believed that the state lottery was rigged. He also believed you only win the lottery if you have purchased a ticket in an area where the population is about a thousand people. Once a week, he drove from Norfolk, Virginia, down Highway 58, until he reached U.S. 95. Once on 95, he would enjoy driving 95 mph like other road rebels. Exiting at exit 172, he drove about another ten miles to a service station with an attendant named Bill, where he would play his numbers for the week.

"Hey, Bill, how are you doing?" Herman asked.

"I am doing just fine, Herman. And how are you today?" Bill asked.

"I am great, Bill."

"Would you like your usual?" Bill asked.

"Yes, sir," Herman assured.

"Five-five-seven. Boxed, exact, and fifty/fifty."

"Herman, why do you drive all this way to play numbers, if I may ask?"

"Well, Bill, my left palm was itching, and you know what that means!"

"Well, are the numbers special to yah?"

"Yeah, they spell KLP if you look at your phone."

"Oh, that is different. What does KLP mean?"

"Kelly Le'Mour Palmer, that's my wife's name," Herman explained.

"Why you never bring her with you?" Bill asked.

"Because she is military and she does not want to drive the distance."

"Have you ever asked?" Bill inquired.

## Kubuki Love

"No. And let me get an easy pick for the big game. I am feeling lucky."

"You should," Bill encouraged.

"Maybe next week, Bill. This time is my time. I am using it to think and relax, while I visualize how I am going to spend this money once I win this lottery. Now give me one of those PowerbBall and Mega Millions easy picks. Okay, Bill, I will see you later, but it won't be next week."

"Why, Herman, will you be on vacation?"

"Yeah, spending the lottery winnings after I hit the jackpot!"

Bill laughed. "Awe, go ahead with that. I will see you next week, Herman."

"I am telling you, Bill, my palm is itching," Herman said as he walked out the door.

"Hey—hey, Herman, which one of those tickets are you going to win the big bucks from?"

"All of them, man. All of them."

"Well, what are the numbers on those easy picks, because I want a vacation, too. I would love to get away from here for a while."

"Well, I tell you what, Bill. Write down the numbers and when we hit, we are going on vacation. Just me, you and Russell."

"We gon' bring Russ?" Russ looked up with those hunting dog eyes and barked, because he heard his name.

"Yeah, Russ is coming!"

"Okay, Herman, I will see yah later."

Herman got back into his car and drove back to Norfolk, singing along with a Neo-Soul CD he'd made. Before long, he was right back home where his trip first started.

"Kelly, I am home," he yelled from the door.

## Kelly Speaks

"Marsha, I am telling you, girl, this brother is fine! He is nothing like Herman. He works out on a regular basis and his stomach—wow!! Eight-pack!! I almost faint when I see it. I just want to run my tongue across it!"

"Girl, you're so silly. Where did you meet this guy and what is his name?" Marsha asked.

"I met him at the super center, and his name is James."

"James? And what do you mean he is nothing like Herman?"

"Herman has a stomach, Marsha!"

"So!!"

"And he wants to have sex with me all of the time."

"So!!"

"So? Marsha, I almost get sick when he is on top of me doing his business, sweating and grunting all over me. But it's when our stomachs touch that really makes me wants to throw up."

"Kelly, I can't believe you just said that. Females would kill to have a husband like Herman. Hell, I would trade Dillion for Herman any day! Dillion's ass doesn't do shit but work, eat, and sleep. I wish he would give me a stiff one every now and again. He and I only get down one, maybe two times per month. And that is depending on how much time off he has."

"Is that it, Marsha? Herman would fuck me every night if I let him. I wish his sex drive was like Dillion's. I could live with only having to do it once a month."

## Kubuki Love

"Girl, you are so shallow! You don't know what you have! You have a rare gem and you're treating it as if it was an ordinary, worthless rock."

"Who Herman?" A gem?" Kelly burst into laughter.

"Okay, laugh it up if you want to. But you'll see. My mother always said, 'Find a good man who is unhappily married and you'll find a fool as his wife.' My momma didn't raise any fools.

"She also said, 'The values of today's women are gone—far gone! They are into money, material things, and microwaves!' "

"Microwaves?" Kelly questioned.

"Yeah, because they don't cook home-cooked meals anymore; everything is microwaved!"

"Herman is forty-two, Marsha! He farts all day, everyday! The guys at work call him Poopie Johnson. But James, he is a hottie. I don't see anything wrong with him. He is as close to perfect as it gets. After our workout at the gym, I flirted with him and I even snuck a feel of his ass."

"Girl, you felt his ass? Ooooh, Kelly, you married and God don't like that."

"Marsha, the Lord is my shepherd and he knows what I want! The Bible says that!"

"No, it don't! It says that the Lord is my shepherd, thy shalt not want."

"This is also true, Marsha, because I shall not want Herman after I have had a piece of James."

"Girl, you better stop it and go home to your HUSBAND."

"After tonight, I will be James's new wife to be."

"Kelly, you are going to see James tonight?"

"Yes, I am."

"What is Herman going to say?"

"He isn't going to say nothing, because he doesn't know! And he thinks I have Bible study tonight. Why are you so concerned with what he will say, anyway?"

"So, what if he goes to Bible study and you are not there?"

"He never goes to Bible study, so that won't be the case."

"Girl, I hope you know what you are doing, because you got a good man and all he wants is a good woman."

"Marsha, I know what I am doing. James is sweet, and after dinner tonight, we will take this a step further."

## Herman

"Kelly, I am home, Kelly! Kelly?"

"What, Herman?" Kelly said, sounding irritated.

"I was just letting you know I was home." Herman explained.

"Why?" she asked.

"Because it is the husband thing to do, Kelly, that's why!"

"The husband thing to do is to go to Bible study with me tonight. Are you going to do that?"

"No, and why do I have to do that?"

"Herman, do you realize that there are only women from our church that go to Bible study? None of the "BROTHERS" (Kelly throws her fingers in the air to say quote, unquote) are ever there. It is always the wives only. Herman, will I get what I want?"

"Kelly, guess what it is going to be tonight?"

Kelly eyes grew wider and a smile came across her face. "What, Herman?"

## Kubuki Love

Herman said, "I am going to tell you what my daddy told my mother when she wanted something badly. 'Your eyes may shine and your teeth may grit; I don't care about your wants because you ain't getting shit.' "

"Herman, that is not funny! Well, I'm going to Bible study. It would be nice if you went."

"Kelly, I will go when they start saying something. Every time we go to any service, they always end up talking about something other than the Word. Like something that happened to them earlier in the week. It is like the pastor talks one minute of Word to every one hour of stories and fillers. No, I am not going to waste the rest of my night sitting up there with a bunch of women who have nothing better to do but to open the Bible, and talk about their crummy week!"

"Well, if that is how you feel, Herman, then why do you go to church?"

"I go because I need to go for me, not for anyone else in that building. And I also go to hear the Word when it is said without being watered down."

"Bye, Herman, I will see you when I get home!" Kelly starts toward the front door.

"Okay, but aren't you going to take your Bible? You are going to Bible study, right?"

"Of course, where else do I go on Tuesdays?"

"I don't know where you go when you leave here, but I trust that you are where you say you are."

"Bye, Herman!"

"Kelly?"

She turns before walking out the door. "What, Herman?"

"Where is my kiss?"

Kelly returns to kiss her husband. As she turns to walk out, he smooches her behind.

Her neck snaps. "Don't do that!"

"Why not? It is mine! Ain't that what your Bible says? So, when you get home tonight be ready to worship!"

Herman smacked her on the ass again when she turned to leave. Kelly pouted as she walked out.

Herman grabbed himself a beer and the remote; then he turned to his favorite channel. After about thirty-five minutes, Herman thought, *You know what? I think I will go to Bible study tonight.* He rolled a joint, grabbed his coat and headed out of the door. He hopped in his midnight blue 1984 Pontiac Grand Prix, turned his ignition and put in his Michael Franks *Tiger in the Rain* cassette. He lit the bud and sang along with the track that was playing.

## Kelly

Kelly pulls up to the restaurant. She digs deep into her purse to retrieve her cell phone, then dials Marsha's number.

"Marsha, I'm about to go in, but I am very nervous."

"You should be. You are about to commit adultery!"

"And look, Marsha, before I left, Herman smacked me on the ass, *twice!*" Kelly emphasized.

"He is supposed to, Kelly, he is your husband and you should let him, despite the fact that you don't approve of anyone feeling on your butt. That is what men do. They like to smack their lady's butt. It is a man thing."

"Well, I still don't like it. I don't care what anyone says!"

## *Kubuki Love*

"Kelly, I am not going to preach to you about how to be a good wife. I got Bible study tonight, and you should be there yourself instead of gallivanting around with James."

"You are right! You shouldn't preach because you're not married yourself. I will call you when I am on my way home." Kelly turned her cell phone off and went into the restaurant to meet James.

Inside the restaurant, James sat patiently waiting for Kelly's arrival. Tall, slim, and fair-skinned, he stood to greet her. You could see his well-sculpted body through the fitting clothes he wore. That excited Kelly to see a young tenderoni. That's what she called them back in the day.

She became so excited and boldly moist. She said to James, "What do you say to making dinner quick?" Then she gave a seductive grin.

"Okay then, let's order," James added.

"Why don't you order for us?" she suggested.

"Okay, I will. The lady will have the baked chicken with alfredo and steamed broccoli; I will have the catfish with double fries."

Kelly flirted with James the entire time. She hadn't had the opportunity to be this free in a long while.

The waitress brought the food. Her name was Jamie. She encouraged the couple to enjoy their meals. Kelly blessed the food before they both dug in. "Amen!"

James started with the fries. He didn't like cold fries, so he would always eat them first. He explained to Kelly why he ate his fries first whenever he ordered them.

"One, two, three, four . . . twenty-three, twenty-four, twenty-five . . ."

James touched the fish with his index finger with every number he counted, then he stuck the fork into his catfish, and before he could indulge, Kelly asked, "What was that? What are you doing counting before you eat? Is that something that you do as well?"

"Only before I eat fish," he said. "It is something about the smell of fish, or when something smells like fish, that triggers something in me that nearly frightens me. But I like fish!"

Kelly was amazed and the look on her face said exactly that.

"I have to count to twenty-five before I can eat it; then I just go right to it so that I am not interrupted, which makes me count again." James started counting again. Kelly wanted to ask another question but decided against it, so James could eat and they could be on their way.

Dinner lasted only an hour and they headed to James's place for an evening she would never forget. Kelly knew she only had about three hours total to play with, because that was about how long Bible study lasted.

James poured Kelly an icy cold glass of his favorite soda because he wasn't a drinker. "You sure do eat a lot of things that are not healthy," she implied.

"Yeah, that is why I workout so I can eat what I want," James replied.

"Take off your shirt."

James took off his shirt at Kelly's request. Slowly, she rubbed his stomach taking in every ripple of his chiseled abs. She leaned forward and kissed them gently. Her tongue toyed with his navel before kissing his stomach again. Her thoughts were thanking the Lord, as if she was at Bible study.

## *Kubuki Love*

James's penis hardened, he placed his hands on Kelly's head. Kelly moved in to caress his reinforced penis. James tightened his ass cheeks and made his dick jump. She began to undress him. She could no longer wait for what she had come for.

James let her take off all of his clothes as he watched her facial expression. She was hypnotized it seemed, and this made James excited. The fact that James was undersized was unimportant to Kelly. Just the lust she had for feeling a youthful, well-shaped body was enough for her.

"Go get some lotion or some type of lubricate," she instructed James.

Off to the bathroom he went and returned with massaging oil. Kelly placed some into the palm of her hand and began to rub his slightly insignificant penis.

"That shit feels good, baby!" James revealed.

"You like that?" she asked him.

"Yeah."

Kelly undressed herself; then pulled James on top of her. She rubbed his dick along her walls, making them wet and ready. James's excitement grew because no woman had ever taken control like Kelly was. Before Kelly could insert James's penis into her, he slowly went down on her.

Her stomach wasn't as flat as his. In fact, she had some flab left from her pregnancy. That didn't bother James. He kept going down until he got face to face with the pussy, and with one good sniff, he began to count. His finger stroked her clitoris with every number he counted: "One, two, three, four . . . twenty-three, twenty-four, twenty-five." He took one lick. Kelly's body squirmed with anticipation.

"Do I taste good?" she asked, right before he dug in to give her pleasure.

James replied, "Yes," and began his count, "One, two, three, four . . . twenty-three, twenty-four, twenty-five." He took another lick.

It took her a second before she realized why he was counting. She felt embarrassed, but he had already begun his feast. He ate so well that Kelly figured that if he didn't mind, then she didn't either. I guess it made up for his size, which now didn't matter to Kelly.

He worked his miniature finisher like he was working with something. Kelly just traced his body with her fingertips as he rapidly propelled his shaft inside her, until every drop of his juices were siphoned from its sump and tossed onto Kelly's navel. All of his muscles tightened and his body jerked as he released.

Kelly stroked his love muscle a few more times, making sure nothing was left in his shaft. Still feeling a little bit of the embarrassment, Kelly was ready to make her exit.

"May I have a rag and towel, please?" she asked.

James quickly retrieved her request. "Are you leaving?"

"Yes, I have to get home. My husband will be looking for me to walk in the door soon."

"You are married?"

"Yes."

"I didn't know you were married. Oh, no, I am going to hell for adultery!"

"No, James, you're going to hell for having a small dick and no moves. Oh, shit, did I say that aloud?"

"Yes, you did, with your funky-ass pussy! Get the fuck out my house, ho!"

## Kubuki Love

"Ho? Who you calling a ho, you black-ass vegetarian?"

"Vegetarian?"

"Yeah! NO MEAT!! You little dick, no moves having, simple muthafucka!"

"You liked it, with your flabby ass! Now run home to your husband, ho. I feel sorry for him, having to put up with your stank ass!"

Kelly stormed out of James's place fussing the whole way back to her car. "How dare he talk to me that way," she cried.

"Bitches are scandalous," James exclaimed; then he yelled, "FLAB ASS!" before he slammed the door.

Kelly turned her cell phone on and it beeped to alarm her that she had a messages waiting. Eight missed calls Kelly read on her phone's display. "Damn, who was blowing up my phone?"

It was Marsha. The text read: GIRL, HERMAN IS HERE @ BIBLE STUDY! & HE SMELLS LIKE WEED. HE WAS ASKING ME WHERE YOU WERE AND IF I HAD SEEN YOU?

"Hello?" Marsha answered.

"Marsha," Kelly said.

"Kelly, where you been. I have been calling you all night. Are you home yet?"

"No, I am just leaving James's house."

"What are you going to tell Herman?"

"I don't know yet. But let me tell you about what just happened with James."

"What?"

"James called me a flabby-ass ho with a funky pussy!"

Marsha contained her outburst of laughter. She almost spit in her hand trying to hold back.

"He did what?"

"Yeah, with his little-dick ass. He could not even perform."

"What? Are you saying he wasn't worth it? And why did he go off on you like that?"

"Because I never told him I was married, and when I told him I had to go because my husband would be waiting, he said I made him an adulterer and he feels sorry for my husband."

Marsha started laughing.

"Why are you laughing?"

"I . . . don't . . . know." She laughed.

"Marsha, it is not funny! Besides, how does somebody that fine have morals?"

"I can't believe that, Kelly. He said your pussy stank?" She laughed uncontrollably.

"Look, I will tell you everything tomorrow. I'm pulling up to the house."

Between giggles, Marsha mustered the strength to say "bye."

As Kelly turned into the driveway, she noticed that all of the lights in the house were off. She walked in and turned the light on and noticed that Herman was sitting there in the dark, listening to Michael Franks and smoking weed.

Before Herman could question Kelly about her whereabouts, she walked over and apologized to Herman for getting upset. She explained that she decided to go to the local bookstore instead of Bible study, because she needed a little space to clear her mind and think.

"Baby, I am kind of tired, so I am going upstairs to take a shower and go to bed."

"Okay, baby." Herman kissed Kelly's forehead; then he asked, "What is that funky smell?"

"What smell?"

## Kubuki Love

"I don't know, but it smells like fish." He stood up and began sniffing around to locate the scent. He got closer and closer to Kelly, but she began to back away, making facial expressions, indicating that Herman was acting weird.

"That must be some good weed, baby, but I am really tired and would like to shower before hitting the sack."

"Kelly, where you been?"

"The bookstore."

"I don't see any books?"

"You can read the books right there in the store."

Herman searched Kelly with his eyes up and down, then sniffed her again. He reached for Kelly's waistline as to pull her waistband. Kelly was caught off guard; she pulled back and ran up the stairs.

"I am on my cycle, Herman!" she yelled as she bolted up the stairs to the bathroom.

When they retired to the bed, Kelly was silent and she kept to her side of the bed, not wanting Herman to bother her. She just wanted the night to be over.

"Kelly, I checked the trash."

"And?"

"And I didn't see any tampon wrappers."

"So, it was a false call, Herman."

Herman just stared up at the ceiling. "Okay, baby."

Kelly fell asleep quickly.

Herman got out of the bed because he couldn't sleep. He went downstairs to grab a beer and watch himself some television, until he felt sleepy. He flipped through a few channels until he stopped at the news.

"And tonight our lottery jackpot is two hundred thirty-one million. Now for our pick three, the first number is five! Our second number is five! And our third number is . . . seven! Five-five-seven; that is the winning number for the pick three!"

Herman was so excited he didn't bother to listen to the other numbers. He was adding in his head how much he had just won.

"I told Bill!!" he celebrated. Herman took his tickets to the store to cash in, only to find out . . .

*Kubuki Love*

## Monessen
## BGL the Beginning!

It was 3 AM and I was still a tad bit tired from my long drive from Norfolk, Virginia to Monessen, Pennsylvania. I had arrived in town slightly after 4 PM, but my uncle wasn't off from work; so I thought I would just chill at one of the local bars until he arrived.

There were only a couple of people there, mainly employees. I ordered a 151 and coke. It didn't shock me that the drink was only a dollar, because I was used to the cheap liquor prices in these small towns. I laid five dollars on the counter and then asked the bartender for two more. I left the change there for her to keep.

As a hustle, my uncle worked at this particular bar to bring in some extra cash for his family. His shift started at seven and lasted until closing. He showed up about fifteen minutes before his time to work, but the crowd of locals didn't show until 10 PM.

I grew tired of sitting in this bar not really knowing anyone but my uncle, until a familiar face walked in, taking the available seat next to me. We hugged and shared smiles. The night began to pick up as we talked and caught up on old times. It seemed as if we had talked and drank for hours, but it had only been an hour and a half.

My uncle was busy behind the bar serving drinks and fellowshipping with frequent customers, so much so, that he barely had time to give to me. So, I tried my best to make my own company.

"So, Nate, how long is you in town for?"

"Only for tonight," I responded.

"When did you get here?" she asked.

"At four," I told her.

"Why are you leaving so soon?" she asked.

"Well, I am just stopping in before heading to Detroit. This is a halfway point, so I just stopped in to see my family, get some rest, then leave for the D," I explained.

"Oh, I understand," she comforted me. "Hey, baby!" she said, as she hugged some girl that came up from behind us to say hi to her.

"Lelah, this is Nate. He is from Detroit, but he lives in Virginia. He is in the military."

"Hi, how are you?" Lelah asked.

"I am fine," I told her.

"What brings you here?"

I explained to her that my favorite uncle stood behind the bar.

"Is that your uncle?" She smiled a smile I had never seen before. Something hid behind her smile and she wasn't telling. She grabbed my uncle's attention for the moment.

"Hey, Blink, come around here and sit with us for a minute," Lelah summoned him.

"I can't right now, but I will in a few when it slows down a bit."

That time never came. Before you knew it, time had come for the bar to close and Blink, along with his cousin Lomax, began escorting drunken people out of the bar. One guy was even tossed to the street with force because his drunken ass didn't want to leave the establishment.

"Come on! Your ass has got to go! No more drinks Muthafucka!" Lomax yelled. "If you don't get the fuck out, I am going to throw you out and then I am going to rob you!"

Lomax was getting pissed off and the liquor was getting me hyped. I wanted to fuck somebody up, simply because my ass was leaving town soon. Lomax was a little older than my uncle and me. He was also a body builder, and he constantly wore this I-am-not-to-be-fucked-with look upon his face. Lomax grabbed ahold of that man and tossed him like he weighed nothing! The man slid along the concrete and came to a stop near the curb.

Once the last gentleman had made his exit, we locked up; then Blink and I went around the block to another bar called Jabb's. That bar had already closed, but Blink used his charm and street credits to gain us access. There were many more people inside than what was at the previous bar. Blink ordered a round of drinks for him and I, then quickly went to mingling with friends.

I kind of sat at the bar alone for a few minutes, until Nicole came to sit beside me and introduced herself. We quickly moved past the small talk and began to talk more on a subject that we found common to each of us. This bar had to be historical for this neighborhood; it was embraced by earlier woodworks and antique lighting. The bar itself was well-crafted with hand carved wood and seasoned bar stools.

Nicole wasn't my usual style of woman, but she seemed nice. My aunt always told me to refer to plus-size women as pleasantly plump, so not to insult anyone. Okay, so I will take her advice on that one.

Nicole being pleasantly plump wasn't what I was accustomed to; however, she was a genuine person. Blink felt that it was his duty to keep the drinks coming and I didn't complain. I just nodded a brief "thank you" in his direction and continued on with Nicole.

"Let's Dance," she asked.

"I don't dance ." I tried to tell her, but she wasn't buying it.

"Come on, I will teach you," she said.

I was getting to be too intoxicated to argue, so I got up on my feet and made my way to the dance floor. I stood in the same spot the entire dance. Nicole was kind of loose; she backed that thang up on me and caused me to lose my footing. I stumbled backward, almost falling, and Blink burst into laughter.

"Is she too much for you?" he yelled from across the room.

I regained my composure and held on this time. She wound her waist, generating closeness between us. I wasn't moving much, but I knew that this was dirty dancing. We began to get stares from the onlookers; one person even cheered us on as if we were a couple. It was known that I wasn't a local because everyone there knew everyone there. I was to be initiated into the "new guy club." I came into town probably once or twice a year, so for a while, I was always considered the new guy.

Nicole's butt rubbed the front of my jeans; she knew what she was doing. I just went with it . . . I figured no one here knew me, besides Blink. Little did I know the alcohol was giving Blink the giggles. He laughed as hard as he could. It was an uncontrollable laugh as he watched in amazement how Nicole was grinding on me. He was even starting to crack fat girl jokes!

"Hey, Nate, it looks like you're in BIG trouble!" He laughed. The people around him began laughing.

## Kubuki Love

One thing about Blink is, once he gets on a roll, he can't stop. He spit joke after joke. The crowd around him laughed so hard that they were slobbering. Nicole was in a zone and she heard nothing, but I couldn't ignore the laughter that came from across the room. I even laughed! She asked why I was laughing, so I lied and said that I was thinking about that guy my cousin tossed out of the last bar.

"Who?" she asked.

"Lomax," I said.

She knew him as crazy and notorious for whooping ass! She stated that there was a rumor going around that he used to do work for an assembly of organized crime personnel.

"Ten Minutes!"

That was their way of saying last call. I guess the law was everyone had to be out of the establishment by a certain time. Quickly, we returned the bar to grab a last drink before closing of the bar. I paid for that round and I ordered the strongest top-shelf liquor they had. Nicole asked could we give her a ride home.

By the time I made it to the truck, I was good and drunk. Blink owned a pickup truck with one bench seat. It was one of them small pickups and we squeezed in like toes in socks.

"I am going to take you two to Nate's car. He has enough room in there for the both of you," he snickered.

She offered for me to stay at her house. Besides, I didn't want to knock on my aunt's door this time of the night; and I wasn't staying over Blink's because he had a huge dog that liked to fuck with people while they were 'sleep or trying to sleep. Along with that, I would have to endure the jokes until he fell asleep. I took her up on her offer to crash at her house. I really didn't want to drive because I was pretty messed up.

We finally made it back to her house, which was actually right around the corner from the bar. Blink could have just dropped us off at her house; then picked me up in the morning. They called this area of Monessen, the projects, but compared to Detroit projects, these were luxury apartments.

Damn, I was tired and the alcohol began to make me fatigued. I kicked back on the sofa and tried to make small talk while Nicole put on some soft music. The more I lay back on the couch, the more I wanted to rest. Nicole noticed me dozing off, so she politely asked me to come upstairs to lie across the bed. That 151 really got me tripping; she had to help me up the stairs I was so wasted. I plopped on the bed and she returned downstairs. I said to myself, "Finally, a man can get some rest before driving to Detroit in a few hours." I knew I was in no shape to drive anywhere.

Nicole appeared back in the room where I laid. She removed my shoes, socks, shirt, and pants; I just let her. I lay still in my underwear like I was too drunk to move. I felt Nicole's hand on the outer portion of my drawers, rubbing, caressing, and moving my penis with her fingertips. That shit felt so good! Again, I lay still, allowing my dick to get hard so she could take every inch of it between her thick lips. I imagined her mouth being as warm as a heated blanket at Christmas time.

She could tell that I was really into it by the way my soldier stood at attention. Gently, I arched my back so that she could ease my underwear off. I could once again feel her hands playing with my erect johnson. The anticipation of her sucking it was getting the best of me, so I gyrated once and nearly let out a moan. Her plump fingers were creating magic. I was thinking, *Damn, this girl got some skills!* I had never had any girl play with my dick the way she did. I was concentrating in order not to cum right there between her fingers.

Nicole stood over me and began to dance sensuously along with the music. I couldn't believe my eyes. She had climbed her big ass up on the bed and danced like we are in some type of film. I thought I was the victim of some prank! She continued her dance as she rubbed her breasts and wound her waist; she even placed one of her nipples in her mouth.

I was laying there with a smile on my face when all of a sudden, I said, "Girl, you better get you big ass down before you fuck around and fall."

I could not believe I said that shit out loud and it made me laugh. I could image her falling and breaking something. She ignored me and continued her performance, if you will. I closed my eyes and envisioned her being some famous actress. I could feel her moving, and my lack of concern just allowed her to finish going through the motions. Her knees bent and she attached her paws to the wall where there should have been a headboard.

Something was smelling like used fish grease up in that mother; she lowered herself onto my face before I knew it! That is what I get for closing my damn eyes! She gyrated as I squirmed like an animal caught in a trap! Her enormous ass had me pinned—I couldn't breathe! I tried to push her off, but she thought I was rubbing her ass. "Lord," I asked, "if you get me out of this one, I promise I will not ever drink again!"

The thick lather of her juices coated my chin and cheeks; her pussy tasted like cheap orange juice! I fought to keep my mouth closed, but I was suffocating! Finally, she dismounted and climbed on top of my shaft and I nearly asked out loud "where is my dick suck?" but I didn't, and I was very disappointed that she didn't suck it. I felt like a victim! Here it was, she had snuck in, putting her pussy in my face, hadn't sucked me off, and now because of her size, she could barely spread her legs around my hips to ride me; however, she did the best she could with what she had.

I had to switch the position and hit it from the back because I had vengeance against her after the stunt she'd pulled, and I was upset that she didn't give me a blow job. I felt that every girl deserves to suck my dick. I have a sexy dick! I'm sorry, but I can't help it. And it's not my fault I was given an eye-pleasing pecker.

I worked my pleasure tool into her from the rear; I worked that dick like nobody's business. Nicole's screams of pleasure filled the little bit of night air we had left. I stroked that cat like it owed me something. Her pussy was as deep as it was wide . . . in my book, if it is as deep as it is wide, then that made it a ditch! My mind was set on digging it out. I gave her my daddy long stroke: this is where I would pull back until the tip was at her vaginal entrance and then I would shove it in, trying the gain access to her stomach. With my hands tightly holding her waist, I pounded daddy-long-stroke-style like I wouldn't see pussy for twenty-five more years!

I have to say I was giving it to her! I am sure she will remember this night whether she says I was the bomb or whether she says I beat it up! My balls slapped her clitoris with every powerful thrust. Every passionate sigh fueled my quest to go deeper, harder, faster! I pulled back swiftly, ready to dig deeper into her crouch area. As I thrusted forward, she lunged forward clutching her ass cheeks and said, "Wrong hole!"

"My bad!" I said, and went right back to digging her back out!

Sweat plummeted down my chest toward my navel. I knew I was giving it all I had. With my muscles jumping out of my chest and arms, I held on for dear life as I reached a point of sexual satisfaction. Once I released my grip of her waist, she fell as if she was lifeless onto the bed. She sighed as if she was glad I had finished my business.

Damn, I was tired and my adrenaline was pumping at the same time, causing some weird feeling inside of me. I had just prison-fucked her as if my name was Tyrone! My emotions were in an uproar. I felt like I'd just beat that pussy thoroughly as I lay beside Nicole until my drunken ass went to sleep!

She woke me up with another piece of ass and no breakfast. Although I thoroughly enjoyed some morning, or shall I say afternoon, tail, I was kind of feeling like *what kind of big girl don't cook breakfast. No sucky and no breakfast!* I began to question myself.

What was I doing wrong? My game wasn't as airtight as I thought! I was done; I was getting out of this place! I was hungry as hell and all she wanted to do was fuck the skinny new guy! I gathered my things and left.

I arrived at my aunt's house and she asked if I had stayed with Blink; and I said no, I was with some girl named Nicole.

"Nicole?" she questioned.

So I describe her and my cousin, John, blurted out of nowhere. "OH, snap. I know who you were with! You

are a nasty buzzard! You were getting it with Nicole?"
He laughed.

I was thinking, *Why him and Blink clowning me
over getting hit off last night?* I know John went to bed
with dry dickeness. Fuck 'em both. I got me some and
she wasn't going to see me ever again.

So I loaded my vehicle and headed up the road to
good ole Detroit, Michigan, feeling a little more confident
about big girls. My aunt had instructed me to call as
soon as I got in, because she knew I'd partied all night
long; and it was a danger to drive such a distant on a
bunch of alcohol and little rest. I comforted her by saying, "Yes, ma'am."

As I drove down the road, ever so often I would pull
my waistband from my waist and look at my dick. I
wanted to make sure I wasn't carrying any illegal meat
crawlers to Detroit. I asked myself if I would ever fuck
a fat girl again. Some say there ain't nothing like a big
girl's loving! I say, if it is a trick, then she better suck a
dick!

Good ole Monessen; the home of the Greyhound.
Maybe I will have better luck on my next visit! Well,
onward toward the Motor City to see what I can get into there.

## Refined Black Man
## 16th Chapter

**Dymond**

With sweaty palms I approached her . . . She looked half Black and half Puerto Rican. We met for this first time in a local Laundromat. I loved her complexion, style, long hair, but that wasn't enough. I had to have more! I wanted to explore her personality. I wanted to know her. I wanted to say to her, "Can I go down on you?" My body wanted to embrace her body; my heart said be direct with her; my mouth took all these emotions, compiled and scrambled them to say to her, "Hello." I began to have thoughts of how corny that came out and how she was just gonna reject me on the spot.

"Hi," she said in return.

My heart became at ease, but I hadn't prepared a comeback to that.

"Umm . . ." Damn, I am stumbling for words now, how uncool is that? She smiled. She flashed her eyelashes once, revealing her shyness. Speechless is what she left me. "Can I start this over again?" I asked because I was fouling this up and I wanted it to come out like I meant it.

She laughed. "Sure," she replied.

"Hi, I am Dymond!"

"Hi, I am Valerie," she said, smiling from ear to ear.

"May I give you my number with hopes that you will . . . I'm not good at this."

She took the clothes from the washer and tossed them into the dryer, depositing two quarters. I checked out her behind parts and a slight smile came upon my face. Valerie was petite, but her rear was quite meaty. I could only use my imagination for the remainder, because she was wearing baggy sweats. All I know is she had an onion!

## Valerie . . .

"Dayuuum, he is handsome. But he is old enough to be my father. Oh, shit, he is coming this way!" she said.

"Hello," he said.

I thought that his voice was sexy. He kinda sounded like one of those beer commercial guys. He was very well-manicured. His hair was cut short and he was wearing Cool Water, my favorite cologne. My nipples hardened. I thought he was cute the way he was stumbling over his come-on lines. Not bad for an older man. He was refined!

I could tell a lot about him by the shoes he wore. My mother told me you can always tell a lot about a man by the way he keeps his hands and feet. First: men that make good money have new shoes or shoes that look new. Second: his thumb is a reflection of his penis size; and if his hands are clean, then so is his pecker! It may look as if he doesn't work, but that's not usually the case, it shows he is caring.

"May I start this over again?" he asked.

"Sure," I replied. Before I knew it, he had handed me his number and was out the door, putting his clothes in his car. He drives an Acura. Hmmm . . .

I just smiled and held the number to my nose, smelling his scent. My mind drifted into passiondise— yeah, I said passiondise: that's passion paradise . . .

On my windowsill, I sat in a long, button-down shirt that was his, sipping wine. The room was overlooking the waterfront of Virginia Beach, and I'm listening to some Brian McKnight. He walks over and rubs his soft hands across my shoulders, massaging my lust for a good back rub. His touch lost altitude and began caressing my breasts; my nipples became erect.

He kissed my collarbone; I stood upon request. His hands took a tour reaching my ass; he cupped it with both hands and began kneading. My tongue danced worldly about his chest. My panties began to soak; I could feel his hard penis pressing against my belly button. I wanted it! I kissed lower and lower until I took him in my mouth through his pants.

His hips gyrated gently . . . I wanted more! I reached in and pulled out what I craved! Usually, I don't give gentle kisses below on the first encounter, but I know older men love oral sex.

He was just the right size—not too big, not too small. I knew I was gonna enjoy this! I work him hard with my hands, caressing his ass, while my mouth suckled his juice! I could feel his knees begin to weaken . . . I could feel the passion escape his shaft. I wanted him to cum. I moaned. Again I moaned, and again. He tightened his grip on the back of my head, pulling me in, faster and faster, until—*AAANNNN!*

The buzzer went off on the dryer and took me out of my daydreaming.

Do you want more? Check out KLP 2

*Rory Leon*

## KUBUKI LOVE POETRY

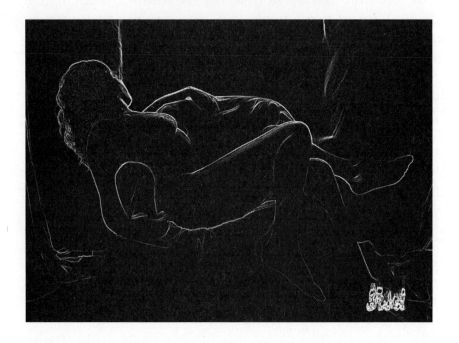

*Kubuki Love*

## Reality of My Weakness

Damn, after all the years that have passed, you are
still looking good.
I never envisioned you coming back around my neck of
the woods.
How have you been?
Me? It is all to the good
Trying to hide the obvious the best that I could.
I feel a little awkward, but I'm not letting this moment
pass.
I remember all those times I straight waxed that ass!
It was young love not knowing the love I had.
A diamond untouched hid in my pad
A diamond uncut lay in my hand
A diamond, my best friend that is loyal to her man.
The reality of my weakness has now come to pass
Because all I can think about is waxing that ass.
Are you married? she asked.
Yeah, but what does it mean?
Know that marriage isn't always what it seems.
Yeah, I know what you mean,
I am married as well, but right now it doesn't mean a
thing.
Aw, shit, it was about to jump off
I embrace her and it felt so soft . . .
I'm going to hell for this! My soul will be tossed!
But care isn't a factor when love is aloft.
It is for me a dream come true.
But what the fuck am I going to do?
Too late to start crying the blues.
Off comes the shirt; then came the shoes.
The pants, underwear, and then the socks

All barriers are gone between cunt and cock!
Once she started, I can't stop.
She reached with her hand and cleaves to my cock!
On my brow sweat rippled,
Her tongue gently tracing my nipple,
Slightly, it tickled
All the while, still holding my pickle.
The reality of my weakness
Overtaken by her sweetness
And all of the things she used to do to me
She did them all again just as keenly.
Kissing inches of my body yet so gently,
Pleasure filled, descending increasingly
Through touch she would speak to me
Rendering me speechless yet peachy
Loving on me, to her, came so easily.
Passion is a way her heart could win me!

The reality of my weakness strengthened real quick.
She knows what I like with her mouth around my
dick.
Up and down
Slurping sounds
From the top of the shaft to the base of my balls she
licks.
The feeling rumbles deep within the jungle of my pow-
erful prick.
I began to think, how could either of us return home to
our spouse?
That thought instantaneously faded as cum flowed
within her mouth.

I didn't think the day would come when I would see
her face again.

## Kubuki Love

Merely memories until now . . .
Visually a reality of seeing an ex-girlfriend.
Entering her with grace, the stroking gaining its
ground!
This pussy is so good the dick feels as if it will never go
down.
Slow down! she whispers.
I want to enjoy this piece of ass . . .
It is feeling so good inside I don't know how long I will
last.
The gyration is slow but intense; she firmly squeezes
my ass
Deep beneath her walls, I feel the wetness blast.
She moans
I moaned
We moan as one.
I thought the night was over. In fact, it had only just
begun.
Young lovers all over again is what we had become.
We fucked until her walls were swollen and my dick
was raw and numb!
Her sweetness is my weakness.

*Rory Leon*

## Get Your Mind Right

Sunflower seeds are nasty to me
I don't eat okra and I don't like peas.
However, things that I do eat are nourishing to me
It is wet, sweet, and very juicy
Soft but firm, and I find it tasty
The light coat of fur irritates me
When I bury my face in it my vision is blurred.
I like it
I love it
This tasty treat
Grows on trees, not between knees.
It is called a peach.
So get your mind right!!!!

## Loyal Pussy

There is a such thing as pussy loyalty
And it needs to be incorporated in the life of a person
like me.
Don't get me wrong, I am picky!
When it comes to loyal pussy, I want mine prissy!
Let me explain what I mean when I say it must be clean
And at least 15 years beyond the years of green.
I want that pussy tight, clean cut and ready to fight
The likes of Mr. Good Dick to the wee hours of the
night.
I want my nuts upset because they have to work over-
time
Exploding within the nappy dugout lubricating the spine
With every thrust from behind
It counterattacks like Laila Ali in her prime.
There is no ducking and dodging
No weaving and bobbing;
It is strictly blow for blow.
Head to head combat is homosexual so I'll just go
Head to camel toe.
Loyal pussy will be there when I need it, no matter
where I tell it to go.
My personal Tamarillo.
When my movement is protrusive
It is not illusive
The prissy pussy's loyalty brings me to a conclusive ex-
clusive
That it is easy to fall for this pussy acoustics
Entertaining as a hootenanny
Is the efflorescence of this pootenanny.
Trustworthy, loyal, and the best kept secret

Rory Leon

Best enjoyed when freshly scented, waiting to release
its secretion
So smile as I take a while to unwrap this hidden beach
And reveal to Mr. G. D. perfectly ripened peach.
Move that shit
Take this good dick
Except it as the best you ever dealt with
Twitch within, never befriend this muscle that pro-
trudes ripples around your tits.
Make me pull him out and rub it against your clitoris
And put it and pull it out again. Until you convulse
and sweating like
You're feverish
That is what I call good pussy
Loyal pussy
Pussy I want to be with
Be next to and sleep with
Cuddle and speak to like it is the weekend
Got my mind tripping like it was the best weed I
smoked
Inhaling every bit of it and never choke
The loyalty of the prime pussy teaches me a new
stroke
Talented as it is never revoked or superseded by the
traditional okeydoke
I am healed from the warmth of this loyalty like a cup
of noodles soup
It feels good beneath my touch like a brand new Lexus
Coupe
I am married to it mind, body and soul
Loyal pussy is so addictive my feelings are out of con-
trol.
I feel the tears fill up the wells of my eyes
But I am too proud to cry

### Kubuki Love

So I hide all those emotions that make you cry
They stay bottled up inside
When between those thighs
I release that cry
Is when loyal pussy just got better
As we lay and cry together.

*Rory Leon*

## Mr. Good Dick

Oh, you know how good dick taste
Use your imagination to determine the taste of great-
ness
Toward the next level you'll elevate . . .
And want not for this Good Dick to go to waste
Lick those lips
Pinch those tits
Feel the twitch between those hips
Wet is the clit
From this Good Dick that feels so monstrous
I'm notorious
You'll feel a rush that is dangerous
From moves and positions which leaves you furious!
Getting next to you is critical
There is no telling what the clit will do
When this Good Dick is being administered so good to
you,
Making feel good the inside of your walls is crucial
It gets so slippery and wet that I might lose traction
Maintaining my grip is my immediate action
Ensuring my stick shift is firmly in place causes a
chain reaction.
Disabling your defense mechanism by an emotional
attraction,
I call that ass waxing
Hovering above your wetness causing myself to hydro-
plane until my tailspin
In a circular motion,
Those curves I am steadily stroking
Until I desire a second wind . . .
Your eyes roll into the back of your mind
It is only a matter of time
224

## Kubuki Love

Until your climax descend its climb
Making you feeeeeel soooooo fiiiiiiiine
There is never a need to lick before I stick
The cause of that would cause multiple organisms until feverish
Sucking that clit like a piece of licorice
Robbing it of all of its sweetness
Licking and sucking constantly until sensitive weakness
Emotionally rendering you speechless
And then when you reach it
There would no doubt in your mind that I would have feasted!
Nonetheless, I feel no need to do that
When good dick has always got my back
Especially when there is a good ass to wax!
Even in the back of a Caddy I Lack
Mr. Good Dick always got it together
No matter whether
You're into whips, chains, wax, lace, or leather
Once you have had Mr. Good Dick it gets no better!

*Rory Leon*

## Peanut Butter-Honey Suckle-Beautiful Light Skin

You are my peanut butter-honey suckle-beautiful light
skin
With gentle soft kisses of butter pecan.
With whispers of desires of pleasing this man
Passion escapes the touches of your hands without
plans.
Trace the outline of my lips with the warmth of your
tongue . . .
I closed my eyes to enjoy what is mentally and physi-
cally fun.
Seductively you tease me, my buttery nipples you
pinch
Then licking slowly the syrup that is placed upon my
chocolate flesh
I am impressed!!!
Your eyes gaze at me while you're licking your lips
Do I taste tantalizing?
Am I making you wet?
Am I that one forget-me-not that you'll never forget?
Am I that first buck earned that never got spent?
I will take you to places that you've gone but never
went!
Bring you back to earth now you're Heaven sent.
You're my peanut butter-honey suckle-beautiful light
skin
You are sexy with your bottom lip tucked in when you
grin.
You are sexy with your hair down and your body em-
bracing the sheets
I get excited when I hear you moan
Ummm . . . You taste so sweet!
Don't move! Let me do all the work

## Kubuki Love

Yeah . . . from your nectar cums peaches-n-cream
Ummm . . . I feel your body shake a little and those
moans turn into screams.
Come, love, enjoy these juices which flows from my co-
conut tree
The strawberries are ripe on the caps of your knees.
Pluck the cherries softly
Now blow them gently
Continue working your magic
I am feeling easily pleased.
Relax my body
Massage that muscle
Stop!
Now that is how you tease.
Slowly now
Ooooh, right there
Here comes my chocolate crème.

*Rory Leon*

## You Deserve Better than That!

You deserve better that!
All that you've done for him, and still your face gets
slapped!!
Not physically but mentally,
Still the pain reins the same deep down for infinity!!!
Put up with it if you might . . .
I know where you would be safer at night . . .
I know what you like . . .
I try not to argue with my lady, I would never hit her
because her I would never fight.
I am about love and love you I will
I am about pleasing you as pleasantly as if may feel.
To me that is
But love is I and I am love, we are one and that is real.
You deserve better that!
Why would anyone subject himself or herself to that
type of drama?
God blesses all of his children and things come back
as they will and that is karma.
Let me rub your pain until it piddles away.
Let my passion be embraced by the softness of your
face.
Hold my hand and lead me into your personal space.
Hold me close and let not go of your sweet embrace.
We'll cry together if that is what it takes.
Allow me to cherish just a brief moment with you . . .
& just for a minute my touch will bring truth!
I was taught how to treat a precious gift that my God
has given me.
I want you!
You are that gift.
Come to me willingly.

## *Kubuki Love*

Be mine until he sees fit
To terminate it!
Then come again and don't quit
I was meant for you to be with!
Let this be a bouquet of roses that brings a smile to
your face when you see me.
Let this be the beginning of things your presences war-
rant that you miss.
Hold me closer to your heart than you would your per-
sonal diary.
Scribe with your passion and love into me your most
secret memories
And together we will share a special something that no
one will every break
I will be yours, whatever it takes!
Because, baby, you deserve better than that!

Rory Leon

## Strawberry Vodka

I want to enjoy you until the very last drop!
Sucking the edges until you scream for me to stop.
Ooooh . . . Damn! I am breaking a sweat!
What I hold in my hand is trying to dry out but I hold
my position and keep that motherfucker wet!!!
Can you feel me? I mean do you understand my point?
I feel your sensuous juices begin to anoint . . .
My body because your body sweats from the cold
I hold you; I filled you with desire until you almost
overflowed.
Then I wait . . .
Will you soothe me?
Will you make me a slave?
Will you love me as I do you?
Will you follow me to my grave?

I hear you call me again so we can start anew.
Crystal clear you appear to me; your effect on me is
overtaxing especially when I'm blue.
I am intimidated by your beauty are you the least bit
surprised?
I am hypnotized again by the sparkle in your eyes.
These events are taking a toll on my body and I began
to fall asleep . . .
I finish the job, wipe my mouth then I inspect my
teeth.
I'd love to love you until my heart begins to leak.
It'll be the best-kept secret that you'll ever keep!
Keep smiling as I stare at the body of your mimosa.
Still framed; still in my brain, as if my mind was a Mi-
nolta.

### *Kubuki Love*

Garnished with a strawberry and sweetly stuck with a pink umbrella.
I am blessed that my lips embrace the rim and caressed such a sexy stellar!

*Rory Leon*

## DSLs

The last we spoke I told you how much I enjoyed those
lips
Not to kiss but just to enjoy your spit
Causing my pump to activate until you quit
Still enjoying every time you moisten your shit
Wishing I was your chap stick
Now put the bottom lip beneath your teeth.
With a girlish grin show me how much you're enjoying
ecstasy.
As your mind pictures me deep inside
Then I take it out to trace the outline
Of those sexy dick sucking lips.
Dumbfounded although I am far from dumb
I am all excited to the point of precum.
I hear you slurping before you sipped
You can't even begin to imagine what I feel
When I am feeling you work those dick sucking lips.
Now that I am a married man
And marry meaning happy in which I am.
It's a sin to indulge in the devils master plans
But the girth of me will soon fill your hands
I don't know whether or not you are feeling me
But tasting me is sweet like revenge
Squeeze every drop out as if you'll never taste me
again
Caress my unmentionables that I have not yet men-
tioned
Show them love with the same attention.
Lift them gently with the fingertips
And journey the hwy to sweet existence!
Now, let your tongue just play awhile . . .
You glance at me to see me smile.

## *Kubuki Love*

I put my bottom lip beneath my teeth.
You tell me that my nectar is sweet
The toes have curled upon my feet
It is passionate pleasure to watch you eat.
You don't quit until you are done
Those dick sucking lips are gonna make me cum.
Again and again until my sump is dry
Temptation is a killer I can't deny.
You work and work it from its limpness
Then you are at it again
Damn those dick sucking lips.

*Rory Leon*

## Reverberation In My Mind

**R**eading through the words escaping the larynx
**E**motions scamper wildly while remaining emotionally attached
**V**ery explicit no matter the consequence
**E**very word said becomes a word that is meant.
**R**umbling through the phrases, grasping it contents
**B**efuddles me every time I wonder what is meant.
**E**verything you say cuts with diamond tips
**R**ipping my heart to shreds while keeping it intact
**A**lways saying that you love me but love can't be spent!
**T**he money doesn't mean a thing if there is no one to spend it with.
**I** feel like I always end up with the shortest end of the stick.
**O**ne, two or three which door do I pick?
**N**oises in my head . . . my mind is playing tricks!

**I**nnuendos are sometimes the hardest to deal with
**N**o Merchant knows the struggles that I am dealing with.

**M**ay I give you just a single uncomplicated hint?
**Y**our wishes are my command; I am putting checks on your wish list.

**M**aybe this is just figments of my imagination said the illusionist.
**I** am hallucinating about fading into the greatest of all distance . . .
**N**ow I sit, just me alone with walls that reminisce
**D**estroying what little is left of the wishes from my wish list.

*Kubuki Love*

## Brown Sugar
(Saccharine Russet Chocolate)

Sweet double brown very unique
Always has been a queen to me
Chocolate beauty a longtime no see
Calm and collective, speaking delicately
Have a smile today, tell God Thank You! Please do that
for me.
Always loving family unconditional
Reverberation in my mind of what use to be
In a time where we should have been one but we were
three
No regrets, wrong place and time chocolate brown sac-
charine
Every time I am with you I want you! You are so sexy!

Remember the time when you feel asleep?
U in my arms resting peacefully?
Soft were your lips when kissing me
Secrets that was held by us so closely
Ever encounter meant so much to me
Touching your flesh felt so heavenly.

Can we do it all again for old time sake?
Hock the ham for some great steak.
Only the two of us participates
Creating what was always meant to be without mis-
takes.
Only the truth remains and I am cleaning the slate
Lust starts all over again it is all on our face
All we need is the opportunity to create
The long lasting memories we can't
Erase.

*Rory Leon*

## I Beg Your Pardon

Hot as a muthafucka . . . My AC is broke
Shit ain't funny and life's a joke.
But things looked good from where I am standing
Supplying the high is so demanding.
Getting high brings reprimanding
Millions of excuses from people panhandling
Bills always keep me scrambling.
My mind is going south, west its landing!
US Air is stale my lungs are constantly expanding
Sometimes I get Down in the Delta and just can't
stand it!
And even when I fall down I get right back up again.
I am weather protected from fair-weather friends
Who mean me well, when needed
Oh well fuck 'em who need 'em
Treat them bitches like bitches are treated!!!!
Before you lay with them you must un-flea them!
Then just flee them
And get as far away as possible before you be them!
Watch closely your rearview until you can't see them
No taillights you don't want to tease them.
Drive by the river, the river of sin
Put one toe in the water but don't jump in.
Getting until trouble always made me grin
Smoking weed made me laugh then I would always
laugh again.
Shit ain't funny and life's a joke
I should be Jamaican from all of the shit I smoked
Murder is an option if I am provoked
Dead silence over the phone the last time we spoke.
Dead beat dad because I am broke
But I always got money to buy some more smoke.

## Kubuki Love

Child neglected the is diaper's wet
Spend until gone no money respect!
Product of my ancestors what do you expect
Smoke until I am high trying to figure out what's next
Fuck the world with no regrets
Why even look in the mail for a child support check
I mentioned I am broke, what the heck?
Here take this middle finger you project chick.
Application after application filled with reject
Don't want no niggas with a nappy neck
Bad-ass grammar and disrespect!
Where in the fuck did I put my smoke?
Shit ain't funny and life's a joke.
I am not liable once provoked
So for now I just kick back and take a toke.

*Rory Leon*

## My Old Friend

It has been years since we last spoke.
We became best of friends once the silence was broke
After all of the catching of a brand new stroke
The one thing that has burned images in my mind is
when my dick made acquaintance with your throat
Like the champ you are . . . never once did you
choked.
Up and Down slurping sounds
Eagerly it poked!
Your tongue bounced around
Steadily gaining ground
My virginity of a non-sucked dick has been gravely re-
voked!
With one hand you took beneath
Lips, tongue and between the teeth
I smacked your hand and whispered, "Don't cheat!"
Lightning fast you began to speak
Removing all ties between hands and meat
"I am a pro at this, I don't need to cheat."
In her girly voice she said to me.
Then back to work she went without missing a beat.

Never before has this happened to me
I was new to this and it felt so sweet
Never have girls rather plump or petite;
Neither the girl next door, nor the ones up the street
Could not stand next to nor even compete
My Old Friend and her astute technique
The way her mouth surmounts my meat
That shit felt so good it lasted a week!
She lapped up every drop! My night was complete
I was feeling fulfilled and she was ever so neat

## Kubuki Love

Holding all of my climax in the well of her cheeks
She swallowed it all and got none on the sheets
Pro-style
Buck wild
She hopped to her feet
Can I use my hands now?
Then she slapped my ass cheek
Damn you're good as I exclaim in shock
I can't believe the way you just handled my cock
My dick was still hard like it was waiting for more
But there was none left to get but my ass out the
door . . .
So home I went still wanting some more
Dick still hard
Ass cheeks still sore
Images racing in my mind like never before
Of this eventful night in consensual porn
If ever actually rated it would be considered hardcore.
But for the record! I have mad respect
I have mad love and not one regret!
Retrospective vibes like disco techs
Vibrant lights, which shines so brilliant
It could light a path of the love for the angriest mili-
tant.
So I thank you, Old Friend, for which you have truly
giving to me
Something that I will remember in my life's entirety
The dreams that I embellish even when not sleep.
An effervescing moment we shared beneath the sheets
A moment, which last forever . . .
Forever you're with me.

*Rory Leon*

## Last Night I Slept Naked

Last night I slept naked, but it wasn't like all the other times.
This time was different
You weren't there . . .
 I tossed and turned,
I squeezed then moaned!
My penetrating device began to thicken on its own.
I began to sweat as if the air conditioning unit broke.
My mind trying to catch the rhythm of the stroke
I placed my hand between my legs and clutched the chocolate dream
It had to be repositioned before it creamed.
Out of respect for myself this time I am going to keep it clean.
Because times like this it is HARD if you know what I mean.

Last night I slept naked, but it wasn't like all the other times.
This time was different.
The bed felt warmer after my dick had stiffened.
Tossing and turning wasn't doing the trick and
My mind gathered a thought of us is when my pace quickened.
Without a lubricant to keep my hand slick and
Now I lay still with a cramp like I am bed stricken.
Balls shriveled and tight
I hope this doesn't last all night
I want to get some rest but loneliness is putting up a fight!

## Kubuki Love

Last night I slept naked, but it wasn't like all the other
times.
This time was different . . .
There was no one to hold me
No one to console me
But no one ever told me
There would be times like this.
No one ever said I would miss your kiss,
Miss your touch,
Miss your hips
Wanting nothing more but to feel your lips
Right now more than ever, with the sweetness of
strawberries and cool whip.
From the smile on my face to the crinkling of my toes
Enjoying the moment as the story unfolds
Wanting no more nights like this, so for the nights to
come, I will be sleeping with all my clothes.

## Kubuki Love Scope

### Kubuki-Aries

You have the ability to make some important break-throughs in your sexual encounters you set your mind to. Do not to get bogged down by your emotions, which may be feeling a bit heavy and stale. Infuse your day with a blast of unconventional SEX. Adopt a new and fresh technique on whatever it is you want your mate to get accomplished in helping you reach your climax. Maybe new perspective is all you need to make your Kubuki Love experience extremely productive.

### Kubuki-Taurus

You may get the feeling that you are rubbing up against bricks today, and more than likely, this is a result of issues lodging deep inside you. Some of these emotions have to do with the constant stress between old and new fuck bodies clashing within your world. This is one of those days in which you need give in to giving a little head. Pieces of your freaky inner being are hitting you straight in the face.

### Kubuki-Gemini

You may be feeling like you are walking on competitive edge. Someonc has tossed you the challenge and you need to figure out how to conquer and be victorious. Use your fancy footwork to juke as you exercise your quick mind to figure out how to keep your composure. Do not to be too stubborn, or you will not get out of the gates. The key is to stay flexible and go with the flow when unexpected events come your way, indulge! Let the freakiness escape. Ride the wild side and taste the victory that is yours. Remember . . . revenge is sweet but victory tastes sweeter.

## Kubuki-Cancer

Your emotions are stable, although there may be an unexpected drama trying to sneak into the equation. Be aware that bitches will be a bit extra volatile today, and though the situation may be calm and cool one minute, it has the potential of being extremely explosive the next. Try to remain centered and not beat that bitch down so that you don't get thrown off course by other people's erratic emotions. You violent muthafucka.

## Kubuki-Leo

Explore your innovative or irrational sexual side. Your emotions are never running counter to this principal, but instead of letting this put a damper on your progress, use this energy to spur you into action. Take advantage of the new relationship that comes available to you. There are incredible resources at your fingertips; don't be afraid to harness this power and use it to your advantage. There are people out there whom love you just the way you are. Take control of your mate(s) sexuality and release the animal that is caged within.

## Kubuki-Virgo

You might just want to stay inside today and not

speak to anyone. If indeed you do decide to venture outside of the relationship, you are apt to run into opposition pretty much everywhere you go. Instead of seeing this as a negative thing, use it as incentive to explore new ventures. There is a strong set of forces egging you on, so act confidently and boldly. Make sure you get your emotions out; otherwise, they will fester on the inside and do more harm than good. You know what? Fuck that!! Be spontaneous. (Today muthafucka) Find someone new today and fuck them just because they let you! The release will do you good.

**Kubuki-Libra**

You may not feel like you are exactly "clicking" with anything today. Indeed, an adjustment needs to be made, either by you, or by the people you are sleeping with, in order for there to be any sort of resolution. Your emotions may be feeling tied to the ground, yet your mind may want to take off into the stratosphere. Dilemmas between whether to take action or stay passive may leave you paralyzed in your own home. Just go with the flow.
The Kubuki Love Doctor prescribes for you a stiff one! Take it how you want it! Drink or dick, you choose! Better yet, just drink dick! The doctor has spoken.

**Kubuki-Scorpio**

Lock into your emotions and trust your instincts . . . sex is everywhere. Unexpected friends may be coming into play to try and disrupt the flow of things, but keep in mind that as long as you stay solid and focused, you should have no problem keeping the situation under control. The actions you take will have a long lasting effect, so be conscious of how you use your energy. Incorporate a bit of excitement into relationship—the old as well as the new. Keep those friends out of your relationship unless they cum to play!

## Kubuki-Sagittarius

You might not be fully appreciated for the wonderful breeze of fresh air you bring to the group. Fuck them haters, go have yourself a drink (maybe a Puck Master). From the time you touch the glass, (hold the middle finger) when you finish drinking, yell "kiss my ass!" Don't give in to negative forces trying to hold you back from expressing yourself fully. Have confidence. You have everything it takes to be successful in whatever you do. If they are not with you, then they are against you. Take a more hood approach—Fuck, Fight or Flee.

## Kubuki-Capricorn

Don't be surprised if things don't go exactly according to plan. No sex for you tonight . . . and you want some badly. Finish reading the contents of this book and proceed to playing with yourself. Unexpected events are more than likely to pop up and disturb the course of action like pre-ejaculation, the phone ringing, or a knock at the door. Realize, however, that these disruptions have a place in your life and that they are occurring for a reason. You might not understand exactly how or why at this time, but that is fine. You don't need to know. Welcome the urge to curse at these stupid new energies. Once you are able to focus again, continue playing with yourself the way you like to until you cum. Isn't life good?

## Kubuki-Aquarius

You're a bit vulnerable, and it may be hard to find shelter from the storm. Maybe it is raining outside your window. Your umbrella is feeling that tingling sensation as a watery-like substance seems to be leaking from within. Comfort yourself, cumming as many times as you very damn well please! Enjoying this quiet evening at home. Don't let other people's unsolved problems infect your space. Differentiate between issues that have to do with you and issues that are simply beyond your control. If you leave the house in this vulnerable state, you may find yourself butt naked somewhere in the fetal position sucking on something other than a thumb!

## Kubuki-Pisces

Unexpected events may be cropping up and poking you in the side. You may get the feeling that there are thorns cropping up out of nowhere whose sole purpose is just to probe your anal cavity. Try to maintain a stable position. Just relax and don't tense up! Think about the end result (LOL). Incorporating sex with relatives into your daily routine is unconventional, but yet exciting. Remember, y'all may go to hell for what y'all just did, so I hope it was good! So, before your emotions start feeling a bit disrupted by the crazy whirlwind of activity, don't get frustrated over that which you cannot control—but control that which

## Kubuki Love

frustrates you. You must have read Literally while your family was in the room. You're nasty!

```
E L C T S G A N U B H E U U W G Z L
O E D O U A P Y U O T O K L A L J A
O O I R G V M L T Z X J I I H U Y X
R P R P A P Z T O S S D O L S B W P
W E E E A Q U R O H O Q A M K S T K
N N F D N B H F V V Q K S A S O L Y
E M I O D E O U M D P V E M I A K L
V I N S R A P L P Z S Z E A M P C L
E C E A I R E S E D F I T E S D U A
S N D M N Z N G A E Z Y N M T V H R
O I B M I E M Q N P I A A Z R R P E
L G L I B B I V U O N L R W A C V T
Y H A E L Y N P T C S T A Z W I Z I
V T C C O R D U B S Q X U U B S W L
I J K K S K E C U I H F G V E L P M
Q W M Z A A D K T K O J Y Y R S C T
O C A N U F S M T U E P A O R D R B
I Z N G T I N A E B X E D U Y E Y U
E Q V B E R E S R U L M 0 H V L A J
Z O R M S N M T H K T R 3 U O U D N
X S R Y O M D E L N E C E X D X H N
R D Z P L F E R O O I E S U K E T N
E U R R C B I M Y I R T T P A N R I
A I Q I E E R V A T A A R V M E I U
L P I N H F R T L A M L I A M R B M
I U K I T V A V P R A O P Y U I Y H
T C Z S A G M B U E I C P C B O P F
Y K T D Y E B P S B R O E I E J P M
H R D R X U Y I S R E H R A Y Q A G
R N G A F L R Q Y E L C G S X C H A
J E . M J P F G D V O U P O I V G X
K H R A U Q Z S O E A B P M M F C D
R Y M G W K R H Y R P V B K Y Y G Z
```

## *Kubuki Love*

| | | |
|---|---|---|
| | Mosaic | |
| 30 day Guarantee | Mr. GD | Refined Black Man |
| Chocolate Crème | Nag | Reverberation Kubukiscope |
| Deluxe | Open Mic Night | Rini's Drama |
| DSL's | Open Minded | Seven |
| Happy Birthday | Paoleria Marie | Strawberry Vodka |
| Hot Tub | Peanut Butter | Stripper |
| Lil Mama | Phuck | Suga and Rini |
| Literally | Puck | The Closet |
| Loyal Pussy | Puck Master | Torpedo Sammie |
| Married men | Reality | You |

## Puck Master

1oz rum
2ozs 151 Rum
Splash of 7 Up
1cup of papaya juice
Splash of lime juice
Blend in blender w/ice, garnish with lime wedge and cherry

## Seven

1cup of Ever Fresh lime juice
2ozs Belvedere
Splash of Grenadine
Sugar the glass's rim

## Punch Drunk

Pour into a punch bowl
Mango Passion Hawaiian Punch
Regular flavor Hawaiian Punch
Berry Limeade Hawaiian Punch
One bottle of rum
One bottle of 151 Rum
Pint of Don Q
Cherries
Sliced and peeled oranges
Sliced strawberries

****must taste while pouring in rum's so that liquor doesn't over power the punch

## Raye J & Brandy

Ruby Red grapefruit juice
2ozs Brandy
Splash of sour
Splash of Grenadine
Shake up and pour over full glass of ice
Pink grapefruit garnish

## Kubuki Love

## *Kubuki Love*

Blue bols
Pineapple juice
Splash of sour
Splash of 7 Up
Splash of Triple Sec
2ozs (your choice of liquor)
Served over crushed ice or blended like a daiquiri

# Hot Like Fire!!!

For this drink you are going to need:

5 tooth picks
Strongest liquor of choice (I prefer 151 Rum)
Mad Dog's Revenge hot sauce extract or Dave's Insanity Sauce!
Saucer or small plate
Cold cola
Crushed red peppers

Place 1 cup of refrigerated cola in center of saucer
Dip each tooth pick into the hot sauce ***caution: not more than 1/8 inch each toothpick***
Place dipped toothpicks around the cup on the saucer (do not touch the cup).
Place 4 separated shots of liquor next to or around saucer.

   1)Start by licking/sucking hot sauce off of a toothpick
   2)Then taking 1 shot immediately after
   3)Next sip cola
   4)Say, "Hot like fire!"
   5)Repeat steps 1-4 until all is finished
   6)Second round, add crushed red peppers to back of hand; lick them off before
        sipping cola say "Hot like fire!" twice.

# Slap Happy!

22oz beer of choice
1/2 cup of liquor of choice
2 people

Each person takes a sip of beer, then sets the bottle down, takes a sip of liquor then places the cup on the table.
Then slap the person across from you lightly . . . continue this process until the slaps get harder and the drinks are disappearing. Winner gets a black eye. And please, no fighting! And no backhands! **pimps are not allowed to play**

# Cherry Bomb!

Fill medicine dropper/needle with liquor (I use 151 Rum).
Squeeze liquor into the cherry.
You may also use this as a garnish for your favorite drink(s).

# Orange Blossom

Remove orange's peel and pull apart orange, leaving it in a circular form/spread.
1oz Triple Sec
1oz Peach Schnapps
1oz top-shelf vodka
Fill medicine dropper/needle with mixture; then inject mixture into each orange wedge.

# W.1.L.L.
# With One Last Love

Splash of Simply Orange Juice
2ozs premium vodka
Simply Raspberry lemonade
Crushed ice
Fill glass with crushed ice. Shake raspberry lemonade with vodka; then pour over ice.
Splash with Simply Orange Juice.

# Detroiter

8oz Tropicana Orchard Peach juice
1-2oz Smirnoff Peach vodka (add to taste)
2oz Peach schnapps
Splash with Faygo peach pop
Garnish with a peach wedge
This drink can be blended with ice into a daiquiri beverage, add peach wedge, and a splash of premium orange juice when blending. 2oz of Smirnoff is recommended.